W9-BSH-742

He swept her up into his arms

"What...what are you doing?" she gasped, trying not to notice that his hard rib cage was pressing into the soft side of one breast, or that one of his arms was wrapped around her waist, the other curled around her thighs.

"Wait and see," he grinned, and began striding around the bank of the billabong along the surprisingly white sand that edged it. Adrianna had frozen in his arms, her hands clenched tightly together across her chest, every muscle in her body taut with excruciating tension.

"Relax," he drawled. "I won't drop you."

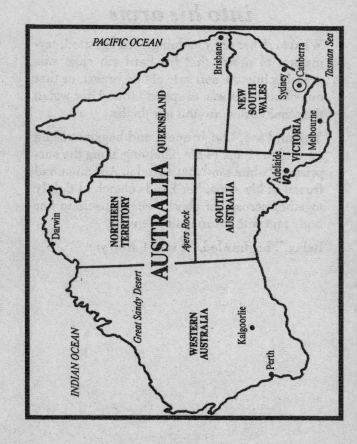

PACIFIC OCEAN

Brisbane

QUEENSLAND

NEW
SOUTH
WALES

Sydney ◎Canberra

Tasman Sea

VICTORIA

Melbourne

Adelaide

Darwin

NORTHERN
TERRITORY

AUSTRALIA

SOUTH
AUSTRALIA

Ayers Rock

Great Sandy Desert

INDIAN OCEAN

WESTERN
AUSTRALIA

Kalgoorlie

Perth

MIRANDA LEE

Outback Man

Harlequin Books

TORONTO • NEW YORK • LONDON
AMSTERDAM • PARIS • SYDNEY • HAMBURG
STOCKHOLM • ATHENS • TOKYO • MILAN
MADRID • WARSAW • BUDAPEST • AUCKLAND

If you purchased this book without a cover you should be aware that this book is stolen property. It was reported as "unsold and destroyed" to the publisher, and neither the author nor the publisher has received any payment for this "stripped book."

Harlequin Presents first edition June 1993
ISBN 0-373-11562-8

Original hardcover edition published in 1991
by Mills & Boon Limited

OUTBACK MAN

Copyright © 1991 by Miranda Lee. All rights reserved.
Except for use in any review, the reproduction or utilization
of this work in whole or in part in any form by any electronic,
mechanical or other means, now known or hereafter invented,
including xerography, photocopying and recording, or in any
information storage or retrieval system, is forbidden without
the permission of the publisher, Harlequin Enterprises Limited,
225 Duncan Mill Road, Don Mills, Ontario, Canada M3B 3K9.

All the characters in this book have no existence outside the
imagination of the author and have no relation whatsoever to
anyone bearing the same name or names. They are not even
distantly inspired by any individual known or unknown to the
author, and all incidents are pure invention.

® are Trademarks registered in the United States Patent and
Trademark Office and in other countries.

Printed in U.S.A.

CHAPTER ONE

THE small red and white Cessna 172 was poised for take-off at the end of the runway, the lone woman pilot waving away the ground attendant. His job completed, the man glanced up and gave her one last long, admiring look.

He had watched her earlier, striding over to the plane, her slender but shapely figure stylishly dressed in a beige trouser suit and a bright yellow blouse. A man wouldn't have been a man if he hadn't been struck by her beauty. Even from a distance, the perfection of her profile was evident, as was the lustrous quality of the white-blonde hair that fell in gentle waves to her shoulders.

Now that he could see her face close up and full on he stared openly at her equally attractive features—the delicate uptilted nose, the sexy, bow-shaped mouth, the very expressive and lovely grey eyes. Eyes which glared at him with definite irritation before their owner masked their expression behind a pair of opaque sunglasses.

The groundsman moved off, muttering. Women couldn't have it both ways, he reckoned. If they did themselves up to attract male attention then they should be prepared to get it!

Adrianna Winslow took a deep, steadying breath, the man already forgotten. She was thinking with some annoyance that she didn't really want to go to Ayers Rock. Sightseeing was not her objective in going flying that afternoon. She was quite happy to just fly.

But red tape demanded a definite flight plan. So she had given them one. Alice Springs to Ayers Rock to the Olgas, then back to Alice Springs.

Simple.

Only things weren't quite that simple, Adrianna admitted as she stared distractedly through the cockpit windscreen down the length of the runway. Nothing seemed simple to her any more.

Alan's proposal of marriage the previous evening had completely thrown her off balance. She needed time to think about it. Time alone, with nothing but empty sky around her. Time to work out just why she was even considering saying yes, when she had vowed years before *never* to get married, *never* to give a man that sort of power over her life!

She frowned as she recalled her first reaction to Alan's question. Heavens, she had been too stunned to speak. He had to be joking, she'd thought. After all, he was already married. To his business!

But then she had seen that he was serious...

Why, she began puzzling, had he asked her now, three years after they had become lovers? There had to be a reason. Alan always had a reason for everything he did.

She could still remember the night when their platonic friendship had abruptly changed into something more intimate. He had taken her out to dinner for her birthday and later, instead of giving her his usual goodnight peck at the door, he had asked to come in.

Looking back, she had the feeling his seduction of her was deliberately planned. And while she could have resisted—her mind and body had *not* been rendered useless with passion—she had sensed a desperation and need beneath his actions that moved her.

Adrianna had never found out what had been behind it all. Perhaps just normal male frustration. But, because their feelings for each other were based on true respect and affection, she had responded to his need and had quite consciously allowed him to carry her off to bed. She had expected nothing really in return, not even physical satisfaction, her one and only other sexual experience having been disappointing, to say the least.

But, surprisingly, sex with Alan had turned out quite well, his skilful lovemaking showing her how clumsy and ignorant her first lover had been. And while her eventual release had hardly been cataclysmic in intensity, it had been pleasant and satisfying.

There seemed to be no way of turning back after that, and Alan had become her lover, visiting her at least once a week. It had proved a comfortable, if somewhat lukewarm affair which Adrianna had never envisaged becoming anything else. Yet now, all of sudden, he wanted to marry her! Why?

Adrianna gave herself a mental shake. Did there have to be a reason, other than one human being's need for the company of another, a need not satisfied by an occasional meeting of bodies in bed? At twenty-eight Adrianna had been living on her own for ten years, and though she had relished her privacy at first there were times now when she ached for someone to just *be* there on a more permanent basis. Couldn't Alan be feeling the same way?

Yes, she decided, he could. And at least, she argued silently, he didn't want children. He had said so.

She closed her eyes, a shudder running through her as the thought of having children evoked memories from the past, memories which she preferred not to think about, memories which still had the power to upset her terribly.

'Miss Winslow! You've already been cleared for take-off,' a male voice ground out impatiently through the radio.

Adrianna snapped back to the present, pride in her normally efficient piloting taking a nosedive. She stiffened her spine and set the Cessna in motion, annoyed with herself for daydreaming at such a time. It wasn't like her to be so easily distracted. Not like her at all.

But then, she admitted ruefully as she accelerated the neat craft down the runway and scooped up into the wide blue yonder, she hadn't been her usual self since Alan had popped the question. She had been confused and disturbed and oddly depressed.

Yet within seconds of leaving the ground she felt a lift in her spirits, an exhilaration. That was how it always affected her, this initial soaring upwards into the air, this moment when the so-called security of terra firma was left behind, exchanged for the nebulous support of air currents rushing over seemingly fragile wings.

Was it the element of danger, she wondered, that caused the addiction to flying, that had made her pursue an amateur pilot's licence after her first joy flight four years before? Was she, underneath her supposedly cool, hard-headed businesswoman façade, really a thrill-seeker?

Unlikely. She hated taking risks in her life, hated the feeling of not being in control.

What Adrianna liked most about flying was not that first rush of adrenalin, but the feelings she experienced later, after the world on the ground had receded from her conscious mind and she was faced with nothing but wide open spaces and endless blue sky. Then she would be enveloped by a mental and spiritual peace that nothing could equal.

It was this mental and spiritual peace she desperately needed today...

She angled the small single-engined plane away from the airport and into a wide sweeping circle, deciding to take in an aerial view of Alice Springs before heading over the mountains to the south and across the desert to Ayers Rock.

She leant sidewards and peered down at the township below, and slowly shook her head. Alice Springs wasn't at all like she'd expected. She had pictured a harsh frontier town, choked with heat and dust, not this green, tree-dotted replica of Sydney suburbia. It was hard to believe that the ordered settlement below was smack dab in the dead centre of Australia.

Apparently they had had a bumper year with regard to rainfall, the normally dry Todd River actually overflowing its banks several times. The town wasn't usually so lush, the locals said. So Adrianna conceded that she wasn't seeing the real Alice Springs at all. Though Alan had been right in his assessment of the tourist situation, judging by the number of motels she had spotted that morning during her drive around the town.

'There's plenty of money passing through the Alice,' he had told her over dinner last Friday in Sydney. 'Plenty of money to buy your Adrianna brand of exclusive Australian fashions. I'm flying out myself on Monday to tie up a site for one of my own stores. Why don't you come along and have a look, see if you can find a suitable spot for one of your upmarket boutiques?'

So Adrianna had flown to Alice Springs with Alan, confident that he would never advise her badly. He had his finger on the fashion pulse, his record for success impeccable during the years she had known him. At the relatively young age of thirty-one he already owned and controlled a flourishing rag trade business, not to mention a chain of quality menswear shops in every main city and large town in Australia.

He had helped her select a boutique site yesterday—in a small but central arcade—and she had tied up the lease then and there. Then Alan had successfully negotiated his deal. Adrianna recalled glancing across the table at him as he studied the menu last night, and thinking how much alike they were, how much in common they had. He had looked up suddenly, seen her watching him, and smiled.

Had the same thoughts struck him too? Had his proposal of marriage been a spur-of-the-moment decision?

Adrianna didn't think so. Alan was not a spur-of-the-moment sort of person.

With a jolt she realised she had been holding the plane in a continuous circling pattern for ages. She flushed as pride in her powers of concentration dropped another peg. Anyone watching her from the ground would be thinking she was mad! Which perhaps she was, to even be mulling over the matter. Marriage was not for her, no matter how much she and Alan had in common!

She quickly straightened the highly manoeuvrable craft and set a south-westerly course, resolving to forget about Alan's proposal for the next few hours and just try to enjoy herself. She had committed herself to going to Ayers Rock, and it was, after all, supposed to be worth seeing.

But to say that Adrianna enjoyed her flight to the Rock was a long way from the truth. She had flown into Alice Springs at night, so she hadn't really seen the surrounding countryside. With Alice Springs so green she had expected the desert to have sprung to life as well. So as she gazed at the landscape unfolding before her eyes she was quite shocked by what she was seeing. Apparently the rain hadn't reached this far south, or if so its effects had been quickly swallowed up by the hot sands, for she was being confronted by the most awesome, endless expanse of flat, dry, hot, red, wretched land she had ever seen. Not a speck of appreciable grass in sight. Not a decent tree, a river, a house. A forbidding, frightening frontier.

She dragged in a deep breath, then let it out with a ragged sigh. 'Heavens,' she muttered. 'What am I doing, flying over this godforsaken place?'

She tried a laugh, but it came out sounding like a nervous squeak. She swallowed, but there was a tight constriction in her throat, a fluttering in her stomach that wouldn't go away. This unfamiliar feeling of fear soon brought a countering rebellious surge, and she clenched her teeth hard in her jaw.

Don't be ridiculous, she told herself. You're no more at risk here than you are anywhere else in the air. Besides, you've paid good money for this flight. Make the most of it!

Her self-lecturing over, Adrianna did settle down slightly, even to almost appreciating the primeval power of the land below her. There was no denying its overwhelming size, its brutal beauty, its ancient grandeur. But she doubted she would ever feel entirely comfortable with putting herself within grabbing distance of its pitiless bony hands. How could one survive, she wondered, if abandoned to such an environment? Death, she felt sure, would come slowly, and very painfully.

So she tended to keep her eyes straight ahead, finding comfort from the familiarity of the sky. Though even the sky was different from what she was used to, the darker blue having a brittle-bright harshness that pierced her sunglasses and made her look down every now and then.

Oh, the joy, the relief, when on one of these occasions she saw a bus streaking along what she supposed was a road, red clouds of dust billowing out behind it. She wasn't alone at all!

The eventual sighting of Ayers Rock in the distance was the final distraction from any further feelings of fear.

'Wow! That's really something!' Adrianna exclaimed aloud.

And something it certainly was. The world's largest monolith, the last remnant of what had once, billions of years before, been a mountain chain, it rose from the desert, majestic and incredibly solid, mute testimony to the incomprehensible dimensions of time and the incorruptible forces of nature.

Adrianna had no idea how big it looked from the ground, but as she drew nearer its enormity awed her. As did its colour—a glittering bronze on top, deepening to a burnished red on the sides.

The strangest sort of feeling washed through her as she approached the Rock. It was humbling, but at the same time uplifting. Adrianna didn't find it surprising that people came from the four corners of the earth to look at this wonder, this concrete reminder of the permanency of their planet.

She waggled her wings as she flew over, waving to the many tourists struggling to climb up the formidable incline. They all stopped, smiled and waved back, and she felt a brief but startlingly intense burst of happiness. It surprised her at first, till she accepted what lay behind it: that, much as a person could take pleasure in something by him or herself, the pleasure was much greater when that something was shared.

The word 'shared' lit up like a headline in her brain. Wasn't this what she had had been missing in her life? Wasn't this the one part of marriage that definitely appealed to her? How satisfying it would be to have Alan always there to share things with, her troubles as well as her successes. Already they shared a good deal. Why not the rest?

It made sense—solid sense. Adrianna decided then and there. She would accept Alan's proposal. She would marry him!

With the weight of indecision lifting from her shoulders, she instantly felt better. Only then did she realise that this was what had been depressing her— her uncharacteristic lack of direction. It was good to feel in control again, to know where she was heading.

A light laugh bubbled up through her nicely shaped mouth. I'll tell you where you're heading, her newly happy self said. To the next wonder of the world!

And with a relaxed smile and the automatic skill of a pilot who had over five hundred hours' flying to her credit, she swung the Cessna away and set her course for the Olgas, the smaller sisters to Ayers Rock. She could see them in the distance, looking like a handful of lavender-coloured marbles, though she knew from reading her tourist brochure that up close they would look much larger and assume an orange-red or yellowish glow, depending on the time of day.

Adrianna was over the huge rounded boulders within minutes, and they were just as fascinating, though not quite as impressive, as Ayers Rock. She circled over them a couple of times, half reluctant now to turn the plane for the flight back to Alice Springs. She had technically chartered the plane for the whole afternoon, a tankful of fuel giving her a range of over six hundred miles. If she went straight back, she would be throwing away three hundred miles' worth of pleasure, just because she felt slightly nervous of the territory she was flying over. Which was pretty pathetic, she decided, never having been one to give in to irrational fears.

So she set a northerly course, resolving to fly a hundred and fifty miles that way before heading for home. She could see a mountain range in the dim distance, which she reasoned was probably the Macdonnell ranges that led right into Alice Springs. They would do for a turning point.

But she came to the mountain range so quickly she decided they couldn't be the Macdonnells, a decision backed up by the sighting of some more peaks on the horizon. She headed their way, enjoying the terrain more now that there was the light and shade of frequent ridges and hills, and the occasional tree and smattering of green on the plains. The sun was beginning to sink in the sky, and a glance at her watch told her it was after three. Once over the ranges she would turn east and head for Alice Springs. She soared over their relatively low height with ease, and was glancing back over her shoulder at them when disaster struck.

What actually happened she had no idea. One second she was flying happily along, the next there was this awful reverberating thud. The back dipped first, then shot up as the nose dropped, the plane plummeting downwards in a deadly spin, its front propeller pointed straight at the ground.

Panic came quickly, and stayed, joined by a wild surge of adrenalin that had Adrianna searching frantically for some way, some hidden skill that would let her escape the certain death she was facing. Those long-forgotten hours of acrobatic flying that were compulsory for all learner pilots came back to her in a jumble. She struggled with the controls, fighting to get the nose up, the wings steady. But her hands were shaking uncontrollably, her stomach in her throat, a burning in her chest. The only plus in the horrendous situation was that the mountains were now behind her, giving her another precious thousand feet with which to avoid the seemingly unavoidable.

Then without warning, without knowing how she had done the impossible, the nose limped upwards, the wings shuddering to a semblance of being level. She was still going down, still going to crash. But she had a chance, with the ground rushing towards her looking blessedly flat.

It wasn't.

The front wheels hit a hump in the sand within seconds of touching down and ricocheted upwards. Adrianna's heart and stomach went with it. 'God help me,' she prayed.

The plane had somehow spun round and was charging towards the base of the mountains she had just passed. It bucked and leapt a crazy path with the brakes virtually useless. The wheels were never on the ground long enough to grip. The crazed craft was gradually losing speed. But not quickly enough.

A cliff face loomed up in front of the windscreen, a head-on collision inevitable. The impact was bone-shattering, but only lasted a couple of seconds before everything went black.

It was dark when Adrianna came round. Dark dark. She couldn't even see her hands before her eyes. But even without seeing them she knew they were trembling. Her whole body started trembling. Her worst fears had materialised. Not only had she crashed, but she had crashed somewhere in that ghastly decrepit desert without anyone in authority knowing exactly where.

Bile rose into the back of her throat and she bent forward, sure she was going to be sick. But she forced her nausea back down, calling on that emergency supply of courage people sometimes found in moments of crisis. Panic and hysteria hovered around the edges of her mind, but she pushed them to one side, telling herself that it couldn't be time for her to die just yet. If it was, then she would have perished in the crash.

She said a little prayer of thanks and set about examining herself for damage. Her hands still shook, but she slowly and methodically felt over her face. No blood, no swelling, just a small lump behind her left eyebrow. She had a headache, though. A bad one.

But one didn't die from a headache, did one?

She stayed where she was, moving first one bit of her body, then the next. There were some parts which, if she could see, were probably bruised, since they were sore. But she didn't think there were any bones broken. It was at this point that she remembered the cockpit light and the radio. Shock had robbed her of her brains, she decided. Cursing herself for her stupidity, she groped forward till she found the light switch.

It didn't work.

She controlled her disappointment with difficulty and groped further, and with a rapidly sinking heart tried the radio. Tried and tried and tried. But there wasn't even a bleep, or some static to give her hope. It was dead. As dead as the plane was, as dead as she should have been.

So be thankful for small mercies, she told herself firmly when panic and despair raised their ugly heads again. They would know by now back at Alice Springs that you haven't returned, she reasoned. Planes will be out searching at first light. And a wrecked plane should stand out like a sore thumb in a desert.

Sure it should, a brutal inner voice piped up. If the rescue planes knew where to look, you blithering idiot!

Adrianna groaned her dismay. Why, oh, why hadn't she radioed in her flight detour? It was pointless to argue that most joy-riding pilots didn't bother with what seemed an officious air-safety rule. The fact was, she had made a fatal mistake which could cost her her life.

But surely, she argued shakily, they would still eventually find her?

Yet even as she kept soothing her fears with logic— Alan was a wealthy man; even if the authorities gave up he would hire all the planes, all the helicopters he could find—a dark feeling of despair took possession of her and her eyes filled with tears. She dashed them away impatiently, only then realising that her sunglasses were no longer in place. She supposed they must have fallen on the floor somewhere. Not that it mattered. Nothing mattered any more...

She started crying with violent, bone-wrenching sobs. This time she didn't try to stop, or tell herself to be brave. It felt good to cry, to let out all the shock and terror that had been building up in her ever since

she had come back to consciousness. And by the time
the sobs had subsided she did feel better. Stronger.
More able to cope with the problems ahead.

A shiver ran through her, reminding her that her
most immediate problem was the cold. It was only
newly spring, and, while the days were nicely hot in
the desert, the nights were freezing. Adrianna shivered
again as she reached for her linen jacket on the empty
co-pilot's seat, dragging it over stiffening shoulders.
She thought about trying to get out of the plane—
since nature was calling—but in the end decided to
try to hang on till dawn. It would be crazy of her to
fall over and hurt herself in the dark after surviving
such a horrific crash.

The dawn came with agonising slowness, worry,
muscular cramps and a bursting bladder making real
sleep impossible and the wait sheer hell. Around five
there was sufficient light for Adrianna to struggle out
and relieve herself. But she was appalled to see exactly
where the plane had finished up, jammed under a
ledge, with a surprisingly leafy tree growing out of
the cliff above and completely overshadowing it. From
the sky the little Cessna wouldn't be visible at all.

She groaned, her despair intense as her eyes travelled wearily along the body of the plane till it reached
the tail. Or at least, where the tail should have been.
Her gasp echoed up the empty grey hills behind her.
Goodness, what had happened to the *tail*? Surely it
couldn't have fallen off through metal fatigue. It
looked like a fairly new craft. She must have collided
with another plane in mid-air, even though she hadn't
seen one. Perhaps the other plane hadn't been
damaged and had flown on to tell the authorities what
had happened, and where? If so then they would know
where to look for her after all.

These thoughts lifted her spirits. Till she gazed around properly for the first time. 'Oh, my God!' she cried softly.

A pale pre-dawn light was streaking the cliffs behind her with an eerie misty blue. But it wasn't this that filled her with dread, but the terrible ocean of sand that stretched ahead of her as far as the eye could see. What if she were wrong? What if there had been no other plane? What if no one ever found her?

She turned away, her eyes brimming. She blundered over to the plane and sagged against it, her head dropping into her arms. But within minutes she had straightened, resolving to spend her energies, not on panic and futile tears, but in finding ways and means to help her survival till rescue came.

First she searched the plane, and was greatly relieved to find a two-gallon can of water, two apples, a thick checked rug and a small tin of cream biscuits tucked under the passenger seat. That, combined with the orange drink, banana and packet of mints she had in her straw carry-all, would at least stop her from dying of thirst and starvation till she could be rescued. She was glad too that she had brought a hat with her, even if it was a rather impractically elegant straw creation which sported a jungle-print chiffon scarf around the crown. With some orange juice and a banana in her stomach and the hat on her head, she set about collecting rocks to make a large SOS out in the open.

The sun lifted higher, a hot ball of heat that sapped her strength and dehydrated her body. And while she was hellishly hot she kept her jacket on so that her arms wouldn't burn. She wished her sunglasses hadn't been totally obliterated in the crash, for the glare was horrendous. The flies were a bother too, making her regret she'd left her insect repellent back at the motel. Perfume and hair spray, she had found, didn't work.

But creature comforts were hardly important at this point in time, she thought, and kept carting more and more stones into place. She had already completed the letters, but she continued making them more definite, thinking that any activity was better than none. She was afraid that sitting around worrying would quickly bring on the hysteria she felt lurking just beneath her surface composure. Twice she heard planes. Depressingly, though, they didn't come near enough to see her distress signal or her frantic hat-waving.

The third time she picked up a sound Adrianna scrambled up on to a high rock ledge. Her gaze searched the pitiless blue sky, but she couldn't see any plane. Gradually, the sound she was hearing became clearer and louder, but it wasn't anything like the drone of an engine. It wasn't coming from the sky either, but from somewhere out on the desert plains ahead.

She shaded her eyes with her hands and peered out into the distance where the escalating heat had turned the sands into what looked like a shimmering lake. It was the first mirage she had actually seen, and she could imagine how they would have fooled many a man dying of thirst.

The sound was coming closer, becoming a definite clang-clang as regular as a pulsebeat. But still she couldn't see anything.

And then she did, her hands dropping from her eyes, her mouth gasping wide as a camel and rider appeared through the haze. They were moving at a quick trot, a swinging cow-bell under the camel's neck responsible for the noise she was hearing. A pack-camel followed behind, strung to the leading animal by a rope, its neck stretched forward with obvious reluctance at being hauled along at such a speed.

Amazement soon gave way to an overwhelming relief, and Adrianna found herself leaping down from the ledge and dashing across the hot red sand towards her rescuer. Her hat flew off on the way, but she didn't care. 'Here! Here!' she screamed. 'I'm over here!'

Her heart pounded as her feet stumbled over half-hidden rocks. But she didn't seem to notice the scrapes to her sandalled feet. The man on the camel had seen her—she was sure he had. She was safe, she was safe. She wasn't going to die after all!

CHAPTER TWO

THE man riding the camel looked startled by her hysterical approach, and reined his animal in with a loud 'whoa!' It responded immediately, skidding to an ungainly halt not a metre from Adrianna, but the camel behind blundered on, cannoning into its leader's backside and almost dislodging its rider from the enormous bedouin-style saddle.

Adrianna stared up at her unlikely knight in shining armour on his equally unlikely steed, unashamed tears of relief welling up in her eyes. But the man wasn't looking down at her. He was glaring back over his shoulder and slowly shaking his head.

'For Pete's sake, Dumbo,' he chided, 'are you deaf as well as stupid? I said *whoa*, not *go*!'

The camel hung its head, glancing up at its master so sheepishly that Adrianna found herself laughing.

The man swung his gaze back to peer down at her. He lifted one large leg over the saddle and slid down to the ground with a surprisingly light landing. 'You have an unusual sense of humour, little lady,' he drawled.

Now not many people called Adrianna *little*, her five feet nine inches being considered quite tall for a woman. Admittedly, she *was* lightly boned and the well-designed trouser suit and yellow silk shirt didn't add any bulk to her curvy figure. But not in anyone's wildest imagination could Adrianna be considered petite. Still, next to this man, any woman might have seemed little. Not only was he excessively tall—six four

22

or five at least—but he was broad and muscular as well.

Very muscular, she judged, mentally stripping him of his bushman's clothes of khaki shirt and faded blue jeans. Her eyes ran down two long powerful legs, then up, till they reached a ruggedly handsome, tanned face and the bluest of blue eyes she had ever seen, eyes that were surveying her from underneath the dusty brown Akubra hat with an equal and rather unnerving candour.

'I take it you're the only survivor?' he asked.

'Yes,' she croaked.

The man sighed. 'So the pilot *was* killed. Poor devil!'

'No, no, you've got it all wrong.'

His frown showed confusion. 'He *wasn't* killed?'

'No...he wasn't...I mean...' Adrianna dragged in a steadying breath. 'I'm the pilot,' she stated. And waited resignedly for the usual male reaction.

It didn't come. There was a slight lifting of his left eyebrow and a muttered, 'Well, well,' as his eyes swept over her again in a swift reassessment. But all in all his reaction was less chauvinistic than one might have expected of an outback man.

'Passengers?' he asked, clearly a man of few words.

'None,' she answered just as succinctly.

A flash of relief crossed his eyes, and she wondered why.

'And you're not hurt?' he went on in that lazily attractive voice of his.

'A few bumps and bruises,' she admitted. 'And my shoulders are a bit stiff.'

'Mine too,' he said, and sucking in a deep breath, stretched his arms wide.

My, but he had a big chest, Adrianna thought,
seeing the buttons on his shirt almost pop out when
his lungs expanded. Big chest, big shoulders, big
hands. Big all over, she fancied.

A flush crept up her neck as she realised where her
eyes had strayed. She whipped her gaze back upwards, relieved to find that her rescuer hadn't noticed
her potentially embarrassing appraisal. His blue eyes
were fixed over her shoulder, staring at the wreck of
the plane.

Adrianna felt quite irritated with herself, not to
mention startled. It wasn't like her to ogle a man
physically. She knew a lot of women did, but she never
had. Alan was a strikingly handsome man, tall and
lean and well-proportioned, but his physical attractions hadn't figured greatly in Adrianna's relationship with him. It was his quick decisive mind, his
strong driving ambition that she found the most ap-
pealing part of his person.

Now here she was, being unexpectedly impressed
by a brawny individual who probably had little more
brain power than the camels he rode. As for drive and
ambition... It was hard to see this hulk of male
machismo having any measurable quantity of either.
He talked slow, moved slow, and by his escalating
silence even thought slow. She decided he probably
made love with the same lack of energy and
enthusiasm.

His eyes swung back to hers, with Adrianna still
rattled by this last thought. For a woman whose mind
rarely dwelt on sexual matters, her thoughts since en-
countering this desert cowboy were definitely getting
out of hand. So he was a good-looking guy with a
great body. So what? she thought dismissively. The
only thing about him that should matter to her was

his ability to conduct her safely back to civilisation, or to stay with her till the cavalry came.

'You certainly are one lucky lady,' he said with a wry shake of his head. 'When I saw your plane go down like a stone, I thought you were a goner. But after I didn't see any signs of fire I began to wonder. I knew I couldn't make it this far yesterday afternoon before dark, so I came over at first light this morning.'

'Came over from where?' she asked, hoping and praying that he meant a nearby cattle station. Though from the look of the surrounding desert-like country-side she couldn't imagine any animals grazing over it with any success. Still, she had read that there were cattle stations in very remote areas now since the advent of artesian bores and other new management ideas.

'I'm camped about twenty miles away. That way...' He pointed back towards the shimmering horizon. 'I left most of my supplies behind in case I needed Dumbo here for someone to ride. It's just as well I did, and it's also just as well there's only one of you.'

'*Me*? Ride *Dumbo*?' On hearing his name said so loudly, Dumbo reefed backwards and almost fell over. Adrianna's face showed horror. 'For twenty *miles*?' she squeaked, aghast. Heavens, she had never even been on a horse, let alone a camel of such obvious waywardness!

The man's face held a sardonic amusement. 'Twenty miles will seem like nothing by the time I get you back home. We're a long way from anywhere here. But don't worry, Dumbo's a lamb. And I'm an expert in-structor. Look, I'll go tie the camels up under that tree for a couple of hours' rest while we have lunch and a siesta, then I'll give you some riding lessons and we can start back.'

He began walking towards the cliffs and the plane, dragging the camels behind him. Adrianna stood where she was for a couple of seconds in shock, then raced to catch up. 'But wouldn't it be wiser to stay here with the plane?' she said frantically. 'It's only a matter of time till I'm found. I know the plane's camouflaged by that tree overhanging it, but I've made an SOS out there in the open with rocks.'

'No one's likely to see it,' he said.

'Why do you say that?'

'Firstly, you're not under any usual flight path. Secondly, you obviously didn't have time to send out a proper Mayday call and give your location, or a rescue helicopter would be here by now. They've had all morning. And by the look of that wreck, your radio's busted as well.'

'Yes . . . yes, it is,' she confessed, surprised by his intuitive and deductive reasoning.

'Want me to make another guess?' he went on drily. 'You took a slight sightseeing detour and didn't radio in your change of flight plans, right?'

'Right,' she admitted unhappily.

His sigh carried exasperation. 'You do realise that's a cardinal sin out here in the outback? People die when they make stupid mistakes like that.'

Adrianna bristled.

'Still,' he continued before she could bite out a fitting retort, 'we're all guilty of taking our safety in the sky for granted every once in a while, me included.'

'You can fly?' she almost gasped, then realised how condescending that sounded. 'I mean . . .' Her voice trailed away in embarrassment.

His expression betrayed definite irritation. 'Flying in the outback is almost as common as driving in a city,' he pointed out sharply. 'I take it you *are* a city girl?' he added, giving her an impatient glance.

'Well, yes, but... Oh, you must be psychic or something! How could you possible know I'm from the city?'

Those startling blue eyes raked over her from head to toe.

'Aside from your making a basic error no outback pilot ever would,' came his laconic observation, 'not too many country girls tog themselves out in pure linen and silk when flying.'

Adrianna stared over at him. He recognised pure linen and silk at a glance? Who *was* this man? She could hardly imagine some roving jackaroo, or drover, or camel trainer, or whatever he was, having such an eye for fashion fabrics. But then he was constantly surprising her, wasn't he?

They reached the back end of the wrecked plane and the man paused, lifting his hat and scratching his head as he stared at the jagged edges of metal where the tail had been. Adrianna stared too, but not at the plane. Her eyes were on the man's well-shaped head, which was covered with attractive thick brown hair cut very short all over. It was not a style she normally liked, but on this man it looked very attractive in a rough-and-tough Army sergeant fashion. Here was a man you just knew you didn't cross swords with, his deceptive slowness probably hiding reflexes that could be as quick as his mind had proved to be.

'Have you got any idea what caused this?' he asked, clearly puzzled.

She shook her head. 'Not really. I thought I might have collided with another plane, but...'

'There wasn't any other plane,' he interrupted firmly. 'I watched you crash through my telescope and there wasn't another aircraft in sight.'

'There wasn't?' She was mulling over what else might have caused her to crash when she suddenly realised what he had said about a telescope. 'Oh! Oh, I see, you're an astronomer!' she exclaimed, pleased at confirming her growing suspicion that her rescuer couldn't possibly be a country yokel.

His laugh was deep and drily amused. 'Sorry to disappoint you. I simply like knowing where I'm going while I'm on walkabout in the desert. I do confess to an occasional study of the stars at night, but I wouldn't know one heavenly body from another. At least...' a slow but wickedly knowing smile captured his strong, wide mouth '...none that are beyond reach.'

Adrianna stiffened, his suddenly admiring eyes sending a warning shiver up and down her spine. 'I thought only Aboriginals went walkabout,' she said in a cold voice, intent on making sure this outback Lothario didn't get the wrong idea where she was concerned. She should have realised that a man as good-looking as this would fancy himself a lady-killer.

He eyed her thoughtfully before speaking. 'In the main, I guess that's so,' he admitted, 'but you can't live out here for as long as I have and not pick up some of their ways. Look, I think we'd best cut the chit-chat short and get out of this heat. You don't have anything on your head, and you'd be surprised how quickly one can get sunstroke.'

With that he took her elbow and urged her to sit down under the shade thrown by the body of the plane. The bush flies immediately surged on to her

still body, making her swat from side to side in the
great Australian salute.

'Little devils, aren't they?' he observed. 'You'll be
pleased to know I have a roll-on insect repellent back
at my camp. Plus some other mod cons.'

'Such as?' she threw after him as he strode away,
the two camels in tow.

'Toilet paper,' he returned with a laugh.

Adrianna cringed. This was going to be a
nightmare! She sighed and watched wearily as her intrepid bushman led his trusty transports up on to the
rock ledge and settled them down under the tree before
returning to squat beside her.

'How much water have you got?' he asked, pushing
the brim of his hat back so that it was perched on the
back of his head. It gave her a clear and close view
of his face, of the strong bones and planes that
fashioned its rugged attractiveness. The lines around
his mouth and eyes could have been premature ageing
from the sun, she reasoned, or the natural result of
his being about the thirty years he looked.

She went to ask him how he knew she had any water,
but stopped herself in time. She wasn't sure yet if he
was a genuinely intelligent being, or merely possessed
of a canny sense of logic and survival. But in either
case she instinctively knew he would have a valid
reason behind any conclusion he came to. And she
wasn't going to humiliate herself further by amusing
him with her pathetic questions.

'There was a two-gallon can in the plane,' she told
him.

'What about food?'

'I've got two apples, a tin of biscuits and a packet
of mints. I had some orange juice and a banana for
breakfast.'

He glanced at his watch. 'Half-past eleven ... If we leave around one, we should make it back to my camp before dusk. But we can't afford to dawdle across that particular stretch. It's mostly salt-pan and there's no water at all along the way.'

Adrianna digested all this for a few seconds without saying anything. It bothered her that she felt so helpless and ignorant. Also that she had to depend on the judgement of a virtual stranger. She had never trusted her future to another human being, and it worried her to have to do so now. 'But isn't your camp due west?' she questioned. 'Wouldn't we be more likely to come across a road and people sooner if we go east?'

'Yes.'

'Then why don't we?'

'Because I'm not sure of the way,' he explained curtly. 'Because I only brought limited supplies with me. And because my dog is waiting for me back at my camp.'

'Oh ...' She could hardly suggest he abandon his dog, or strike out across unknown territory.

'We'll leave a note behind in case a search plane sights your SOS. Though unless they see it soon, the rocks will quickly be covered by blowing sand. Don't look so worried,' he added. 'I've got plenty of provisions. I was expecting to be out here for two weeks yet, but I'll get you home safe and sound in less than a week.'

'A *week*!' she gasped.

He shrugged at her shock. 'It'll take about six days to get back to Dover Downs. But there's a plane there that can take you to whatever city you live in.'

'Sydney,' she told him, frowning. 'Dover Downs... I've never heard of it. Is it a town?'

'No, a cattle station, south-east of the Kimberleys, not far from the border between Western Australia and the Northern Territory.'

'You work there, do you?' When he hesitated she added somewhat caustically, 'When you're not on walkabout, that is.'

His left eyebrow lifted slightly again, and she wished she hadn't used that sarcastic tone. She wasn't sure why she had, except that this man was rattling her as no man had ever done before. Cold sarcasm had often proved an effective weapon for her in the past, when she felt sexually threatened by a man. The difference here was that it was her own sexual awareness that was worrying her, not the man's! Really, except for that one remark about heavenly bodies her rescuer hadn't shown any male-female interest in her at all.

He sat down on the rocky ground next at her, his expression one of total indifference. 'You could always stay here by yourself,' he said, 'and keep brushing the sand off your SOS. They might widen the search for you after a day or two. Are you important enough for them to?'

'My fiancé might think so,' she countered, stung that this man didn't seem to care what she did one way or the other.

His glance went to her conspicuously ringless left hand.

'I... We only decided to get married two nights ago,' she elaborated hastily, an embarrassing heat zooming into her cheeks at this light stretching of the truth. It wasn't really a lie, she excused herself. She would say 'yes' as soon as she got back to Sydney.

Her present companion didn't make any comment, however, and Adrianna got the impression he didn't give a damn whether she was engaged or not anyway.

His gaze had returned to the smashed tail of the plane and he was staring at it, frowning.

Adrianna tried to ignore the pique she felt at such obvious uninterest, but it was impossible. She kept thinking what a mess she must look and began fingering down her fringe, smoothing and turning the ends of her hair under in a rough semblance of its normally sleek, well-groomed state. She groaned inwardly at the thought of her face. Every vestige of yesterday's make-up would have melted off long ago, probably leaving streaks and smudges. She didn't carry a mirror or make-up in her bag, having always hated women who primped and preened all the time.

This thought brought her up with a jolt. What am I doing, trying to look attractive for this man? she thought. I'm an engaged woman. Well...almost!

She lowered her hands and clenched them tightly in her lap, then stared agitatedly out at the desert. 'Alan won't let a stone remain unturned till he finds me,' she insisted.

'Right!' The man beside her stood up. 'In that case, what say I give you what supplies I can spare and leave you to it?'

Adrianna jumped to her feet. 'But...but...I'll die here if no one ever finds me!' she protested.

'True,' he said without a flicker.

She was appalled by his apparently indifferent attitude. 'Don't you *care*?' she asked accusingly.

'Of course I care,' he said in a maddeningly phlegmatic tone. 'But I'm not in the habit of forcing people to do things they don't want to do. I gather from your response to my earlier reference to your delectable female body that you're afraid I'm some sort of wandering sex maniac who's going to ravish you in the desert sands.'

She tried to keep a straight face, tried not to let any sort of guilt show. Little did he know that what she feared most was that she might *want* him to ravish her!

'Let me assure you, lady,' he added with a dry laugh, 'that making love is not high on my agenda of activities for desert crossings. Firstly, the sand is hot enough to burn one's butt off. Then there's a few other hazards such as flies, ants, scorpions, lizards and snakes. Not to mention spikes and prickles. Rolling into a spot of spinifex would dampen even the most determined Casanova, believe me. I don't know about you, but I like my sex between cool sheets, with a freshly showered partner beside me. I also prefer my women definitely unattached, being single myself. So I'm afraid that at the moment, despite your undeniable attractions and a certain lingering dash of French perfume, you just don't qualify.'

Adrianna gaped at him. She wasn't shocked by what he had just said—she was a modern woman, after all—but she hated the feelings of fluster this man kept engendering in her. She was used to being on top of situations, particularly in her relationships with the opposite sex. Now here she was, being thoroughly thrown by this...this *farm-hand*!

She felt the urge to explode into a most uncustomary tantrum, telling him she didn't appreciate such talk; that her sex life was her own business; and that his uncouth self would be the last person on earth she would entertain the thought of cohabiting with—even between those aforementioned cool sheets.

'Well, what do you say?' he went on brusquely. 'Are you coming with me or not?'

Her mouth snapped shut, and she kept it that way while she battled to control her rampant emotions.

Finally she lifted her chin and eyed him with a type of cool reproach. 'It seems I have no other viable alternative,' she said coldly.

'It seems so,' he agreed, an answering hardness steeling those beautiful blue eyes.

Three hours later, Adrianna was regretting her decision to go with him, thinking privately that risking death was preferable to what she was going through. Her head was aching; her shoulders were aching; her bottom was aching; her thighs were aching. Sweat was pouring down her face, her neck, her back, soaking her clothes and making them stick to her in the most uncomfortable fashion. Flies crawled around her eyes, up her nose, into the corners of her mouth. She decided she hated camels, hated the desert, hated the heat; and, above all, hated the man riding the camel in front of her.

Riding lessons, he had said. Huh! He'd virtually plonked her on to the highly uncomfortable saddle, showed her how to hold the reins, shouted 'Up, up!' to the camel, and they were on their way. The only consolation she had was that by the time twenty miles of this torture was completed it wouldn't matter that dumb Dumbo didn't know the difference between 'whoa' and 'go'. They would both sink to the ground in an exhausted, shattered heap.

She glared at the man ahead, amazed that she could have for a moment found him attractive. He was nothing but a bully-boy with no consideration for others, a typically high-handed male egotist who didn't think he had to explain anything to a woman. Within minutes of her agreeing to go with him, he had virtually reduced her to the role of weak, helpless, dependent female, telling her what she could eat, how much she could drink, how long she could rest, what she should wear, etc, etc, etc, without giving the slightest concession to her own intelligence or initiative.

The trouble was that under the circumstances she could do little but acquiesce, or seem like a fool. So she smiled on the surface, and seethed inside. And if she betrayed her underlying resentment occasionally, he pretended not to notice, except perhaps during the incident over her hat. She would never forgive him for that. Never!

It had been so unnecessary to rip two holes in the brim to stuff the scarf through in order to tie the hat on to her head. But he had done so without consulting her. When she had pointed out with sweet sarcasm that the same result could have been achieved by taking the long scarf *over* the brim his face had hardened and he'd said gruffly, 'Not as much shade that way. Nor as firm.'

Then he proceeded to demonstrate by ramming it down on her head and tying it so tight it must have made her look ridiculous. She had fumed under the feeling of impotence that raged within her, unable to stop the fury from showing through in her cold-eyed glare. For a second he had glared back at her, and she could have sworn was about to say something, but at the last moment he had whirled away and stalked off. It had given her a vengeful sense of satisfaction to see that he could be stirred from his annoyingly self-contained persona.

But he had quickly resumed his calm, composed I-know-better-than-you attitude, leaving her feeling just as powerless as before. He was the omnipotent boss in this situation and he knew it. *She* knew it. But it didn't make it any easier to bear, resentment burning through her entire being. Perhaps he sensed the hate-filled glare boring into his back as they plodded along, for suddenly he whirled around in the saddle. 'You OK back there, Adrianna?' he asked.

'Fine,' she smiled through gritted teeth. She refused to call him Bryce, though they had exchanged Christian names back at the plane. She refused to acknowledge that he would ever be anything more to her than a nameless itinerant station worker with whom fate had forced her to spend an unfortunate span of time.

'I want you to grip the front of your saddle,' he shouted back over his shoulder. 'I'm going to break Jumbo here into a trot, and Dumbo will naturally follow. OK?'

'Fine.'

She did as he told her and braced herself for further horrors. Walking had been bad enough, the rolling, rocking gait constantly reminding her of every bruise in her poor battered body. But when the beast below her lurched into the faster motion Adrianna almost died. Her bottom bounced up and down, up and down, till every bone from her pelvis upwards was being jarred with the most excruciating pain. She clenched her jaw hard and held on grimly, determined that not a word of complaint was going to come from her lips. Not a single word! She glared ahead at her tormentor, vowing she would never give him a solitary reason for making her feel more weak and helpless than she was already feeling.

They trotted across the flat, seemingly never-ending plain for over an hour, the salt surface finally giving way to clay, then sand. It felt like a year to Adrianna. She would never have believed she could endure such torment. As she looked dazedly around her at the dry, red parchment of earth, stretching on and on to the depressingly flat horizon, her mind began to wander. She started fantasising about her beautiful home unit back in Sydney, with its wide cool balcony overlooking the crystalline blue waters of Sydney Harbour.

Oh, to be there now, sipping a gin and tonic, relaxing on her favourite lounger, wearing nothing but her silk kimono, her naked flesh feeling refreshed after a cooling shower.

Dumbo stumbled and Adrianna's mind was jerked back to the present, a scream bursting from cracked lips as she began to lose her balance and slip sideways. The enemy was beside her in an instant, pushing her back into the saddle. 'You all right?' he asked gruffly.

'Of course I'm not damned well all right!' she snapped, all her patience worn to a frazzle. 'There isn't a single part of my body that isn't either stiff, sore or sorry. I'm dying of the heat. I've got a rotten headache. And I'm tired and thirsty.' She placed her hands on her aching hips and glared daggers at him. 'I want nothing more than to lie back in a soothing bath full of Radox and have someone bring me a long cool drink!'

A reluctant smile twitched at the corners of his mouth. 'Sorry, can't manage that at the moment.'

Adrianna sagged in the saddle, all the fire gone out of her with her outburst and his understated reaction. Why, oh, why couldn't he at least do her a favour and lose his temper, really lose his temper! She wanted to see for once that he was as human as she was.

Her tired eyes washed over him. He looked too good to be true, his body seemingly immune to the conditions around him. Even the flies let him alone. But of course, he had probably lathered himself with insect repellent that morning, she thought ruefully.

Now his smile had widened, and he was shaking his head at her.

'What?' she snarled.

'You won't want to hear it,' he said, sardonic amusement in his voice.

She lifted her arms wide to encompass her surroundings and herself. 'Could anything be worse than it is? For pity's sake satisfy my curiosity, if nothing else.'

His eyes betrayed a momentary surprise, and Adrianna realised what she had just said. 'I didn't mean it that way,' she groaned.

His laugh was very dry. 'No, I don't suppose you did. But it does make my confession slightly more awkward. I wouldn't want you to get the wrong idea.' He swung his camel and urged it back into the lead, where he stopped and twisted round to look back at her. 'I think I can tell you from the relative safety of this distance.'

'Oh, good grief, what is it?' she demanded impatiently.

The corner of his mouth lifted in a rueful smile. 'At the risk of sounding terribly banal, I was going to say how beautiful you look when you're angry.'

She stared at him as an undermining wave of pleasure flooded through her. But hard on the heels of the pleasure came the disturbing acceptance of her vulnerability to this man. A smile and a tossed-off compliment, and she melted.

But only inside, where no one could see.

'Really?' she said with a cold sniff, and saw the smile instantly fade.

'God, woman,' he scowled, 'you don't know how to take a genuine compliment!'

'Pardon me if I find it hard to believe I look beautiful when I'm dying.'

He made a scoffing sound. 'You haven't begun to die yet.' He went to say something further when a dark frown swept across his face. 'Damn,' he muttered, glaring at something behind her. 'Hold on tight, Adrianna. We have a slight problem.'

And with that he kicked Jumbo into a gallop, Dumbo's subsequent leap into action immediately distracting her from any other thought but stopping herself from falling off.

CHAPTER THREE

ADRIANNA hung on like grim death, her stomach heaving, her mind whirling. What had he seen behind them that had brought such a swift look of panic?

No, not panic, she conceded. A man like Bryce wouldn't panic. Concern and a degree of annoyance was more like it. But over *what*?

If only she dared look behind her.

But she did not. She was having enough trouble keeping her balance with her eyes glued straight ahead.

They were really travelling, each galloping stride of the camels' long gangly legs covering enormous ground. Suddenly the horizon wasn't flat any more, a ridge of sandhills was looming up before Adrianna's eyes.

They hit the soft sand so abruptly that even Jumbo almost lost his footing. Bryce shouted 'Whoa!' but dopey Dumbo hadn't mastered that command yet and careered on. Fortunately Bryce leant over and grabbed the reins, reefing them out of Adrianna's sweat-soaked hands and jerking the animal to a bone-crunching halt.

She gripped the front of the saddle as her body lunged forward, then whiplashed backwards. She closed her eyes and grunted with the pain, though curiosity had her soon twisting around to see what they had been fleeing from.

'Oh, my God,' she croaked. 'Is it a sandstorm?' Her grey eyes widened with horror at the swirling, whirling mass of red dust whooshing towards them.

'Not quite—more a willy-willy. If we can get over this ridge—and the next—we might leave it behind. Sometimes they go back towards the saltpan.'

She steeled herself and sent Bryce a resigned look. 'Then what are we waiting for? Let's head for the hills!'

He looked taken aback for a second, then grinned and kicked Jumbo in the flanks, 'up-upping' both the camels into immediate torturous action.

Luckily, though, he was right. The willy-willy stayed on the salt-pan. But they didn't stop galloping till they were approaching a second line of dunes, these steeper than the last. Only then did the camels slow to a walk, Adrianna sagging across the saddle as the exhausted animals struggled up the incline.

Bryce reined Jumbo in on the crest and waited for Dumbo to draw alongside. 'Almost there now,' he said, and pointed.

Her eyes followed the direction of his finger to land on a most incredible sight. For not more than half a mile away, nestled within a rocky outcrop of low hills, was a small lagoon, fringed by white sands, eucalyptus trees and the greenest of green grasses.

'Why, it's an oasis!' she exclaimed.

'A very temporary one,' he informed her.

She frowned at him. 'Temporary?'

'I don't mean it's going to disappear overnight, but give it a month or two of this heat and the billabong will dry up. It's fed by a creek bed that only runs when it floods up in the north as it did this winter. Twice. We don't have many wet winters like that, though.'

'Well, thank the lord you did this year,' she sighed wearily.

'Poor Adrianna, you must be done in. Sorry I had to push, but you can see why. The salt-pan is no place to linger.'

His unexpectedly gentle tone was more her undoing than all the compliments in the world. Her heart turned over, her stomach contracted, and, worst of all, tears welled up in her eyes.

'Come on, city girl,' he sighed, and took Dumbo's reins, leaving her nothing to do but hold on to the saddle while he led her slowly and quietly down the sandhill. They didn't speak, the silence oddly soothing to Adrianna's shattered nerves.

He wasn't such an ogre, she decided as she blinked away the tears. Not really...

Not at all, she finally admitted. Back at the plane she had asked for his exasperation, what with her patronising him and her prickly, ungrateful, argumentative attitude. Yet, except for the business with the hat, he had remained remarkably patient with her. She was the one who was the ogre, not him.

She shook her head wearily, a silent groan welling up within her. If only he didn't affect her physically the way he did. Heavens, he only had to smile at her and she was all mush inside. It was crazy really. He wasn't her type at all!

The only thing she could think of was that it had something to do with the situation she was caught up in. She had read of prisoners imagining they had fallen in love with their captors, their emotions confused by feelings of total dependence and vulnerability. Was that what this was? Had the crash and the desert stripped her of all her usual confidence in herself, making her susceptible to Bryce's autocratic personality in a way she would never be in her normal life? Or had there always been within her that ghastly feminine weakness she abhorred, the one that made a woman want to surrender her will, her body, and sometimes her whole life, to quite often the most unsuitable male, all in the name of what the female sex foolishly called romance?

A shudder rippled through her at this last thought. It couldn't be, she decided. She wouldn't *let* it be! Alan was the man for her. Alan, who never threatened her peace of mind, who never tried to run her life, who wanted only as much as she was prepared to give, if not less!

'Romance,' she muttered scornfully.

Bryce twisted round and frowned at her. 'Did you say something?'

The blood raced to her cheeks, making her almost glad that her hat was pulled down as it was, for it hid her crazed fluster.

'Not really,' she said curtly. 'I was just giving the flies a piece of my mind.' And she swatted them away all the more vigorously.

'Glad I'm not a fly.'

Again he gave her one of those drily amused smiles and again something deep inside responded, making her feel almost sick. She clenched her jaw hard to stop a returning smile from bursting from her lips, her expression retaining its brittle façade with great difficulty. She was almost relieved when she saw Bryce's eyes darken with exasperation, even more relieved when his total attention was claimed by a black and white dog streaking towards them across the red plain.

'Here, Bully!' he shouted, dropping the reins and leaning to one side, his arms open.

Adrianna was just thinking that no dog could leap that high when the mad animal propelled itself up-

wards, was caught, and gathered in, its adoration of
its master evident in the frantic, feverish licking of
his face. Bryce was laughing. 'Good dog, good dog,'
he praised, lavishly hugging and rubbing his pet.

Adrianna's stomach contracted as she watched
them, her reaction distressing her immensely. Surely
she couldn't be jealous of a man's love for his dog,
could she?

But then she realised her feelings hadn't sunk to
anything quite so low. It was jealousy all right, but
more of Bryce's capacity to show his affection so
openly, so uninhibitedly. She could never imagine
herself doing anything similar, either to man or beast,
and it suddenly bothered her. Oh, how she wished she
could throw off all the inhibiting controls under which
she lived her life. All her fears.

Fears?

She stiffened her spine, her lips pursing together.
Now that was carrying self-recrimination a bit far.
She had never been a cowardly person! All she did
was guard against things happening that could ruin
her life, things she knew she couldn't cope with. She
wasn't really hard-hearted or cold. Underneath, she
was just like anyone else, wanting someone to care
about, someone to care about her.

But she had known many years ago that she
wouldn't fall in love and enter into a normal marriage. She just wasn't capable of surrendering herself
and her life to a man in so total a way, not after all
she had seen and been through. Marriage to Alan was
different. He wouldn't ask her to shelve her career or
abandon her independence. He wouldn't demand that
she change or make unfair sacrifices.

Adrianna darted a rueful sidewards glance over at
Bryce. She couldn't say the same for the likes of *this*

fellow. Any woman in *his* life would have to be a meek, slave-like creature capable of enduring his long absences without a whimper, content to be waiting for him if and when he deigned to return to them. Marriage with a man like that, even without children, didn't bear thinking about!

Yet even as Adrianna's intelligence rejected such a notion she was staring at him, at his wide laughing mouth, at his strong powerful thighs gripping the sides of the camel, at his large male hands hugging the dog. And she was consumed with an insatiable hunger to have that mouth, those thighs and hands on and around and over her hot, tingling flesh.

She shook her head, such crazy, uncontrollable feelings filling her with incredible dismay. Why was she being plagued by this overpowering sexual attraction for this man? *Why*?

'Don't you like dogs?' he asked, giving her a sharp look before letting the wriggling animal slip back down to the ground.

'Why do you ask that?' she managed in a husky voice.

'You were shaking your head and giving poor Bully one of your disapproving glares.'

'Oh...' A type of guilt pricked her conscience. How many disapproving glares had she subjected Bryce to so far? 'Not at all,' she explained in what she hoped was a softer tone. 'I wasn't really looking at your dog. My mind was a million miles away.'

'With some not very nice thoughts, by the look on your face.'

Adrianna swallowed. 'Yes, I...' She hesitated, but he said nothing, obviously waiting for her to explain further. She felt impelled to apologise, but there was a part of her that found such a prospect not only dif-

ficult, but vaguely unnerving. Why, she wasn't sure.
Perhaps it was because she didn't want to show any
weakness in front of this man who was so incredibly
strong in every way.

'I...I was thinking how rotten and ungrateful I
must have seemed to you back at the plane,' she said
tautly. 'And since.'

His eyes showed surprise. But still he said nothing.

'I...I'm sorry,' she managed at last.

Yet he merely shrugged off her apology. 'Don't give
it another thought. You were in shock. You're
probably not usually so difficult.'

She fell silent at that. It made her feel small to think
she had made him suffer for something that wasn't
his fault, especially after all he had done for her. He
couldn't help being attractive. Or having to contend
with a woman who for some reason had unexpectedly
turned into a raving nymphomaniac. It was up to her
to keep her unfortunate feelings in check.

And totally hidden.

Adrianna conceded that while Bryce might not be
the sort of man to force himself on a woman, it could
be a different story if she let him know how vulnerable she was to him. He was, after all, a very virile-
looking man who she suspected wouldn't be easy to
ward off once aroused. And who knew how long he
had been in this desert?

Adrianna decided not to ask him, though. Instead
she adopted a friendly expression and said, 'What did
you call your dog just now?'

'Bully.'

'And is he one?' she asked, smiling.

He gave her another look of surprise, as though he
didn't think her capable of smiling. She wished he
wouldn't keep staring at her mouth so. It was making

her feel uncomfortably aware of him again, which was the last thing she wanted.

She almost sighed with relief when he looked away and down at his dog, who was dancing excitably around the camels' legs. 'He's not any more,' he gruffed, then added more gently, 'Are you, old boy?'

Bully responded with another burst of barking before dashing off in the direction of the oasis. He stopped after fifty yards or so, spinning around and barking demandingly.

'He's very excitable,' Adrianna remarked, grateful for any distraction from her increasingly disturbing feelings.

'Yes . . . It's his breeding.'

She had no idea what his breed was. He was a medium-sized dog, with a stocky body, a long thick nose, small pointed ears, and a weird black and white patched coat. 'What is he?' she asked.

'Half kelpie, half bull terrier.' Bryce chuckled. 'He spent the first six months of his life not knowing if he should muster cows or kill them!'

Bully's strident bark sounded impatient. 'We'd better keep moving before he has a nervous breakdown,' Bryce advised, and resumed leading Dumbo along, talking as he went. 'A chap came through Dover Downs a couple of years ago making a documentary about the outback. He had this mad white bull terrier with him which was the most fearless dog I've ever seen. He terrified the life out of everybody, but one of the station dogs—a lovely black kelpie bitch—thought he was just the ant's pants. She had a litter of six pups a couple of months after the film team moved on, five of them exact replicas of the mother . . . and Bully. My God, the bedlam that pup caused, fighting and scrapping with everything that moved! He was going to be put down till I gave him a reprieve and took him on walkabout last year.'

'And?' Adrianna prodded, intrigued by the story. Or was it the man telling it?

Bryce shrugged his huge shoulders. 'I bonded him to me.'

'How?'

His backward glance slid over her and a shiver rippled down her spine. 'It's amazing what some time in the desert can do to one's personality,' he drawled. 'It takes out all the anger, all the aggression. It makes one look within oneself and find out what one's real priorities are ... Bully finally calmed down enough to find out it was better to be friends with me than fight. After all, there was no one else to relate to, and dogs, like people, need love and companionship. We've been mates ever since.' Again those blue eyes found hers, locking briefly before swinging slowly back to the front.

Adrianna's throat had gone dry. Had there been some sort of message in that penetrating look?

A sardonic gurgle almost broke from her lips as her brutal sense of honesty took over.

Adrianna Winslow, you're becoming far too fanciful for words! she told herself. This desert must really be getting to you. Why should there be any underlying message? The thought that Bryce might be thinking of taming *you*, making *you* his mate, is ludicrous! My God, the man almost left you behind, that's how much he fancies you! For goodness' sake get hold of yourself and stop acting and thinking like some over-sexed adolescent fool! Of course he isn't going to use your enforced time together to try to bond you to him! Of course he isn't planning to seduce you like some lecherous sheikh! He was merely re-

counting a tale about his dog. Good grief, get a hold
of yourself!

All this heated mental arguing did have one desirable result. It took Adrianna's mind totally off her
physical discomfort, which had by now reached
mammoth proportions. She covered the last few
hundred yards of their trek, totally distracted from
her various aches and pains, from the flies and the
heat, not to mention the gritty dryness of her throat,
and the rumblings in her stomach. She was all bitter
self-recrimination and grim resolve, so much so that
it was Dumbo's sudden stooping of his neck that made
her realise they had actually arrived at the edge of the
billabong.

'Do you need help getting down?' Bryce asked,
slipping down to the ground beside Jumbo. Bully was
frolicking in the water around the camels' heads. 'I
want to let the camels have a long drink.'

'I can manage,' she said. ·

But the words were hardly out of her dry swollen
lips before every bone, every muscle in her creaking
body screamed her mistake. She tried to lift one leg
over the saddle as she had seen Bryce do so easily,
but she could barely move it a couple of inches.

'Here,' he ordered, extending outspread hands up
towards her. 'Just lean to one side and let yourself
go. I'll catch you.'

She had little option but to do as Bryce suggested
and have her shattered body caught up by his strong
male grip. He settled her on to very unsteady feet.
When he went to let her go she groaned and sagged.

'Bad, huh?' he asked, holding her upright against
him.

'Mmm,' was all she could say.

'I've got an idea.' Abruptly, he undid the scarf under her chin and took her hat off, throwing it to one side before sweeping her up into his arms. She gaped up at him as he held her close and tight.

'What . . . what are you doing?' she gasped, trying not to notice that his hard ribcage was pressing into the soft side of one breast, or that one of his arms was wrapped around her waist, the other curled around her thighs.

'Wait and see,' he grinned, and began striding around the edge of the billabong along the surprisingly white sand that edged it. Adrianna had frozen in his arms, her hands clenched tightly together across her chest, every muscle in her body taut with excruciating tension.

'Relax,' he drawled. 'I won't drop you.'

Drop her? She wasn't worried about him *dropping* her! Her worries lay entirely in another direction. She held her gaze steadfastly upwards, staring with wide eyes through the dappling shade of the river ghost-gums to the darkening blue sky.

Perhaps he sensed her confusion and fear, for he looked down at her with a sardonic sparkle in his eyes. 'There's a sandbank out here,' he explained, and began to wade into the water. 'It'll be shallow and warm. You can lie there and soak those stiff muscles of yours while I get you a drink.'

She closed her eyes and gave a little moan when he lowered her gently into the surprisingly warm water and let her go.

'I know it's bad,' he soothed, thinking that physical pain had brought the sound from her throat. 'But this should help. Here . . . let me help you out of your jacket. It looks uncomfortable. There, that's better, isn't it? I'll be back shortly.'

Her eyes followed him as he left the water, followed him every step of the way as he walked back to the camels and his camp. And as she watched him she thought she had never seen so big a man move with such smooth grace. There was no side-to-side rolling of his shoulders, no clumsy swagger. Just a long, easy athletic stride that flowed from his narrow hips and compact buttocks, his broad shoulders held square but not tensely, his long arms swinging comfortably.

He walked straight past the drinking camels, past his camp-site, where he tossed her jacket aside, and around to the far side of the billabong down where the water looked much deeper. There he astonished Adrianna by suddenly tugging off his boots, throwing off his hat and plunging in, disappearing completely under the water. Bully danced around on the bank, barking excitedly.

She gasped to a sitting position when Bryce didn't surface immediately. Seconds ticked away, terror holding her frozen. Then suddenly a hand broke the surface, holding a wine bottle aloft like the Lady of the Lake with Excalibur, followed by a triumphant Bryce. 'Success!' he shouted.

He emerged from the water, his wet clothes outlining his impressive body with startling clarity. Perhaps Adrianna should have looked away then, but she couldn't, and when he glanced over at her she was still sitting up, staring at him. 'Now lie back down in your bath like a good girl,' he admonished her across the water, 'and I'll bring you a sample of some perfectly chilled Chardonnay.'

She closed her eyes and sank back into the warmth, willing her body to relax. Her muscles were doing so quite nicely, but her mind—and her imagination—had definite ideas of its own. Her eyes kept flickering open

and darting to find Bryce as he returned to his camp
and went about opening the wine bottle. Finally, with
the bottle and two tin mugs in his hand, he began
striding her way.

A definite lump formed in her throat at the sight
of him coming towards her through the water, his
damp shirt clinging to the broad muscles of his chest,
the beginnings of an amused smile pulling at his
mouth.

'And what do you find so funny?' she demanded,
her inner susceptibility making her terse.

'You have a very dirty face,' he grinned, and
reached out to touch her nose with a spare fingertip.

She splashed her face with the warm water, rubbing
it vigorously before glaring up at him, her skin shiny
and clean. 'Better?' she snapped.

'Much better,' he said, and settled himself down to
waist-level in the water beside her. 'Now all you need
is half a bottle of this inside you and you'll start feeling
human again.' He poured a generous swig into one
of the mugs and held it out to her. 'It might help your
sense of humour as well.'

She took it with a grudging, 'Thank you,' and
downed the whole lot in one swallow without so much
as a splutter or a hiccup.

'Ah,' he drawled, 'I see I'm in the company of an
experienced drinker! Don't worry, there's plenty more
where this came from.' He waggled the bottle at her.
'I buried half a dozen bottles in the sand last year.'
He poured himself a healthy mugful and proceeded
to savour it with considerable sounds of appreciation.
'Hmm... Marvellous... I can see I've found a most
efficient natural cellar. Here, have some more.'

'I don't think...'

'Good idea—*don't*!' he cut in firmly. 'Thinking is the bane of the human race. It causes untold misery. Now drink up, but not so quickly this time. It might not sit too well on an empty stomach.'

Yes, it wouldn't do to get drunk, she thought ruefully. The last thing she needed was to let down her guard with this man. So she lifted the mug carefully to her lips and let the cool wine slide more slowly down her parched throat.

Nevertheless, in next to no time the alcohol hit her system, making her head swim. Initially, Adrianna was instilled with a sharp sense of danger, but the effect of the wine was insidious, gradually pervading her whole body, dulling her conscience and making every part of her feel wonderfully liquid and melting. Any remaining muscular pain receded, her thoughts now of nothing but her immediate surroundings—the beautiful billabong, the warm water suffusing her skin, the man next to her.

Her slightly blurred gaze was drawn to his large, confident hands as he topped up his drink. She watched him lift the mug, watched those strong male lips curl over the rim, watched the wine wash over his tongue and disappear into the dark, moist depths of his mouth. Gradually everything went out of focus for her except that mouth. She saw his tonguetip flick out to capture a drop of wine from the corner of his mouth, and it felt as if it had flicked over her entire body.

Her heart began to pound, her head spinning, her body gripped by the most amazingly intense, incredibly compulsive need. To have this man kiss her, touch her, right here, right now, was not only imperative but essential. She lifted her eyes to his, uncaring that her hungry gaze would betray her desires. This need had no pride, no shame. It drove her to want him to recognise what she was feeling, and respond to it.

Her eyes didn't find his, however, for those deep blue pools were busy with an occupation of their own, staring with narrow-eyed intent over the rim of his mug straight at her chest. Taken aback, she looked down at where her wet blouse was stuck to her breasts like a second skin, the well-rounded bra-less mounds as good as naked before his gaze. As were the rock-hard nipples, jutting through the damp silk like twin spear points.

Oddly enough, his blatant staring at her aroused body had the opposite effect to what one might have imagined. It sobered her immediately, making her realise what a monumentally stupid thing she had been about to do. Alcohol had temporarily sent this crazy sexual attraction spiralling out of control. Of course she didn't want him to make love to her out here like some sort of wild animal. My God, among other things she could quite easily become pregnant. Whatever had possessed her!

With a half gasp, half groan she sank down to neck level in the water, the action sending Bryce's eyes snapping up to hers.

It shocked her to see the lingering lights of a naked desire blazing in them. Shocked her even more to realise that a moment ago, it was what she had *wanted* to see.

But Bryce wasn't shocked. He wasn't even apologetic as he regained control over himself, his smouldering gaze quickly cooling to an icy blue. He even gave an offhand shrug. 'You have a desirable body, Adrianna,' he said. 'Don't expect me not to look. I'm very much a normal male, not one of those effete excuses for men who grace your city offices. I know who and what *I* like.'

He poured the last of the wine into his mug and drained it, then gave her an uncompromising look. 'But don't worry, I'll keep my hands off. Much as I happen to find city women very sexy, I'm not that hard up that I have to force myself on one who's already spoken for. Though to be honest, dear lady...' he darted her a hard, dry glance '...if you want to credibly keep up that air of cold aloofness where I'm concerned I suggest you don't look at me as you did a moment ago.'

Adrianna sucked in a startled breath. So he *had* seen her lustful gaze. Oh, how could she have put herself into such a humiliating position!

There was only one means of escape, one way to salvage some of her damaged pride and avoid a potentially dangerous situation from developing. But it would take every vestige of composure and cool she could muster.

She sat up in the water and lifted her left eyebrow in a sarcastic arch, letting her eyes slide over him in a bold scrutiny. 'You have a highly desirable body too, Bryce,' she returned in kind. 'So don't expect *me* not to look. I'm very much a normal female, not one of those horsey excuses for women who stomp across your cattle-yards. But don't worry, I'll keep my hands off. Much as I find your macho body quite sexy, I happen to prefer my men with a little more spit and polish.' Her nose tilted up with what she considered just the right amount of disdain. 'And I certainly haven't forgotten that I'm an engaged woman. I realise that there are some people who have no loyalty, and who indulge every passing fancy they have, but I'm not one of them!'

For a few seconds there was an electric silence, with Bryce's eyes boring into hers. But then, just when Adrianna was experiencing a prickle of fear—had she gone too far?—he threw back his head and roared with laughter.

She could only stare at him in astonishment. Her clever counter-speech, her cool sarcasm had been utterly futile in putting this man in his place.

Bryce stood up, still laughing, and the water cascaded down off his huge shoulders. 'I'll say one thing for you, Adrianna, you're not boring!' He reached out and took her empty mug, then whirled and began to surge towards the nearby bank with powerful strides, leaving her staring open-mouthed after him. Once on the sand he bent to pat the ever-waiting Bully, then turned back to face her.

'I have to get on with unpacking and making a camp-fire before it gets dark,' he stated matter-of-factly. 'Stay in your bath, by all means. You wouldn't be much use anyway. By the time I explained to you what to do I could have done it several times over.'

Adrianna was still reeling with shock and a sorely damaged ego. To be told now that she was useless, and without initiative, was too much! 'I'll have you know that I . . . that I . . .' she began, spluttering as she tried to get to her feet and failed, her waterlogged clothes and exhausted limbs working against her.

He threw an exasperated glare at her across the water. 'Put a lid on it, will you?' His voice had a harsh, impatient tone he had not used on her before. 'You might be queen bee where you come from, honey, but out here you're nothing but a decorative distraction and a right pain in the neck. So do yourself and me a favour. Just do as you're told from here on in, without argument, and definitely without any of your smart-mouthed retorts, and we'll get along fine. Right?'

'Right!' she ground out through gritted teeth. She folded her arms and sat there, glaring back at him with steely grey eyes.

His grin showed her she was a maiden in the insolence stakes. 'Glad to see you're a quick learner. You never know, once you get off that high horse of yours, we might even become friends.'

He strode off then, leaving Adrianna seething with hostility and humiliation. But at least the scene had totally obliterated any attraction she had been feeling for the man. How she could desire him even for a second she could scarcely believe! He was worse than she had first thought. An egotistical, domineering, typically bossy chauvinist of the worst kind! And he called *her* high-handed. Good God, he left her for dead in that regard!

She watched him go about his chores with the vain hope that he would do something stupid, or clumsy. But no! Everything he did went swiftly and smoothly. The camels were unpacked and turned out to graze. The camp-fire was made, a billy boiled, food prepared. Even the excitable Bully was settled with a large can of dog-food.

A mere half-hour later, with everything apparently done, Bryce returned to stand on the bank opposite her, holding the checked blanket she had found in the plane. 'You'd better get out of those wet clothes,' he advised, 'and wrap this around you.' He dropped the rug on the sand. 'They'll dry in no time near the fire. And before you say it, no, I won't watch. Not unless,' he added drily, 'you want me to.'

Adrianna controlled her temper with difficulty. 'I think I'll bypass that pleasure this once,' she said tartly, and began to dog-paddle towards shore.

He waded into the shallows and met her, holding out his hand to help her stand up. She took it and was hauled upwards, her clothes plastering around her entire body from top to toe as the water streamed downwards. She might as well have been naked, for there wasn't a curve or crevice that couldn't be clearly seen.

She heard his swiftly indrawn breath, felt his fingers tighten around her hand. Her eyes flew to his, but those blue pools were already waiting for her, glittering and unrepentant.

'OK, I looked again,' he ground out, 'and this time it turned me on. What am I supposed to do? Apologise for being a normal male?'

'You ... you said I could trust you ...'

For the first time she saw real anger in his face. 'You can,' was his snarled reply.

'But ...'

'Look, darlin', if a man tried to rape every woman who unintentionally turned him on, this world would be in a right old pickle, wouldn't it? Of course ...' his eyes latched on to the colour flooding into her cheeks, and the way her breasts were rising and falling in a rapid, syncopated dance '... some women prefer the decision to be taken out of their hands ...'

It was just as well, she realised later, that that was the moment a herd of wild camels chose to arrive.

CHAPTER FOUR

THEY came out of the desert, swooping down from the sandhills with red dust flying from their hooves, their leader a huge bull camel making loud snorting noises from his flaring nostrils.

'Bloody hell,' muttered Bryce, a dark frown wiping everything but worry from his face. He abandoned Adrianna and made a dash for Dumbo and Jumbo, who were skittering around under a nearby gum-tree. Grabbing their reins, he tied them securely to the trunk before racing over towards the camp-fire and snatching up a rifle.

'Get out of here, you mongrels!' he shouted, lifting the nose of the barrel and firing a warning shot just over the leader's head. 'Watch yourself, Bully,' he directed to the dog as it flew past. 'That first fellow is mean. Adrianna, for Pete's sake get back into the water!'

But she couldn't seem to move, frozen with shock as Bryce and his crazy dog raced out towards the massive camel. Bully didn't hesitate, charging in and giving the animal a nasty nip on the heels. A large bony leg lashed out in anger, but missed. Bully charged again, and again, till the camel had had enough and retreated a little. The rest of the herd followed and they stood at the camp's edge, tense with thirst and fear. The big bull was swaying from side to side and stamping his feet, seemingly trying to make up his mind if it was worth the risk to try for another drink regardless of the dog and the man.

'Get off with you!' yelled Bryce, firing the rifle one more time. 'There's plenty of water around. Find your own place!' He ran at them and this time the herd bolted.

By the time Bryce turned and walked back to the camp, Adrianna's frozen state had thawed to one of uncontrollable trembling. He found her still standing at the edge of the water, shivering with both reaction and the gathering cold. The sun had well and truly set while all this was going on, and the chill and blackness of night was descending with astonishing speed.

Bryce stood looking down at her, one hand on his left hip, the smoking rifle in the other. His face carried both exasperation and concern. 'Just look at you, standing here freezing to death! Why didn't you get back into the water? At least then you'd have been safe *and* warm.'

'I . . . I . . .' was all she could get out between chattering teeth.

'God!' He threw the rifle down, snatched up the checked blanket and wrapped it around her shoulders. 'Come on, let's get you over to some warmth,' he growled, and guided her stiffening limbs over to the camp-fire. 'Here . . . sit on my bedroll, then you won't get your clothes dirty again. Don't worry about taking them off,' he added abruptly. 'They'll dry in the end. Mine did.'

She sank down to sit on the thick grey blanket, hunching her knees up and leaning towards the heat. She stared blankly into the flames, unmoving, unthinking. The trembling soon stopped, but both her mind and body seemed to have seized up, the incident with the camels having compounded with all the other emotional upheavals of the day to bring about total shut-down.

Bryce crouched down beside her and looped a wet strand of hair over her right ear. A shiver reverberated all through her.

'What you need,' he said firmly, 'is a mug of hot billy tea. I'll just let the camels loose and get you one.'

When he brought it several minutes later she cupped the battered enamel mug in her hands and drank like a robot, without even thinking to thank him.

But Bryce was right. The hot drink did make her feel better. Not good, but better.

The reviving caffeine and the heat of the fire finally forced her mind into gear and her tongue to work, and she looked across at where he was sitting down on a log not far from her, drinking his own tea. He was leaning forward, elbows on knees, looking bleak and oddly troubled. She caught his eye and without thinking what she was doing, smiled. 'Thank you,' she said simply.

His blue eyes were surprisingly hard as they fastened on that smile. 'Don't tell me I'm to be forgiven,' he said caustically.

'There's nothing much to forgive,' she said truthfully. After all, what had he done, except respond to a blatantly exposed female body like any normal virile male? It was her own dark desires that had made the incident seem more dangerous than it was, dark desires that she was determined to conquer. 'I overreacted,' she apologised. 'I'm sorry.'

There was a momentary flicker in his gaze that was almost irritation. It perplexed her. Didn't he want her apology? Didn't he want them to try to be friends, at least on the surface? His eyes dropped to the fire, his handsome face marred by a most uncharacteristic scowl.

A silence descended between them that quickly got on her nerves. She searched her mind for a safe topic of conversation and decided on the wild camels. 'Does that sort of thing happen very often out here?' she asked.

His head jerked up. 'For God's sake!' he said sharply. But when he saw her surprised look his frustrated expression cleared to one of dry amusement. 'Oh...you mean the camel business.'

Only then did Adrianna realise what he had first thought.

'No...not really,' he went on in that lazy drawl of his. 'But the outback has more wildlife than most people suspect, and some of it isn't friendly. You always have to be on your guard.'

'How did those camels get to be here in the first place? I mean...they're not native to Australia, are they?'

Bryce lifted the lids on the two iron pots that were sitting virtually in the fire and stirred while he talked. 'No, they were brought in from Afghanistan last century as pack animals, taking food and supplies to the men building the telegraph and railway systems across the desert. Ironic thing is, by doing so they eventually did themselves out of a job. Once the railway was finished they were no longer needed, so rather than go to the expense of shipping them back to their homeland, their owners let them go. Same thing happened with horses and donkeys. There are plenty of those running loose as well. The camels are the biggest problem, however. Last I heard they numbered over thirty thousand.'

'Thirty thousand!' Adrianna shook her head in astonishment. 'That's an awful lot!'

'Mmm. They're not too popular with some of the cattle men, I can assure you.'

'But you don't seem to mind them?' she pointed out, nodding towards Dumbo and Jumbo, who were grazing contentedly nearby.

'Can't stand those wild ones,' Bryce answered. 'Not only do they devastate the grazing land, but they're totally unpredictable. The bulls are particularly mean at the end of the mating season. Jumbo and Dumbo aren't the same at all. They're domesticated, and trained. Well... *almost* trained. Dumbo's only young. Besides, they're both gelded, so they don't present a problem with their sexual urges. Not like that crazy mongrel you just saw.' He glanced over at her with a self-mocking smile. 'I meant the bull camel, not myself.'

Adrianna saw the funny side of it and laughed.

'You wouldn't find it so funny if you were a man,' he said darkly. 'You women have it easy. You seem to be able to turn your physical feelings on and off like a tap.'

She gulped down the involuntary tightening in her chest. Little did he know...

His sigh was heavy. 'Where was I?' he growled. 'Ah yes... dinner.' He left the stirring and turned to pick up two pale blue enamel dinner plates and two large forks.

'What have you been cooking?' she asked, resolving to get the conversation back on to a less dangerous track.

'A rare couple of dishes! Madam has a choice,' Bryce said drily. 'She can have either beans and wonderfully tasteless dehydrated vegetables. Or wonderfully tasteless dehydrated vegetables and beans. Feel free to take your time with your selection, but be assured that either will tantalise your taste buds as no other culinary delights you're likely to encounter in the Great Sandy Desert.'

It was no use. Even while being sarcastic the man had an incorrigible charm that totally undermined Adrianna's intention to keep him at arm's length. She started to giggle, then laughed outright.

'That's the first time I've ever heard you laugh,' he said, almost accusingly.

'Is it?' She chuckled some more. 'I can't help it. You made me.'

His glance was sardonic. 'One point to me, then.' He handed her a steaming dinner plate and a fork. 'I wouldn't think there'd be too many men who could make you do *anything*, my dear Adrianna.' He cocked his head to one side, and the firelight struck the sculptured planes of his face. 'Adrianna what?' he asked, his beautiful blue eyes softening.

For a second she stared back at him, astonished by the pleasure his warm look evoked in her. Finally she had to drop her eyes lest she betray her feelings, clearing her throat and poking at her food. 'Winslow,' she answered. 'And you?' she added, risking a brief upwards glance.

'McLean.'

'Bryce McLean,' she murmured. 'Nice ...'

'I'm a nice man. As you're basically a nice woman.'

Adrianna's eyes snapped up to his face then, startled by this rather backhanded compliment. For what seemed a long time they just looked at each other. It was not a particularly sexual gaze, Adrianna thought, more a slow steady assessment, a discovery of each other as people. There was interest in the blue eyes looking back at her. Interest and warmth. And yes...a most likeable quality of openness.

Adrianna was the first to look away, a host of butterflies in her stomach. God, she liked this man, really *liked* him! It was a disturbing realisation, for it gave her earlier desire for him a different connotation, one that terrified the life out of her. Lust alone she could probably cope with, ignore, control.

But lusting combined with liking was a different kettle of fish entirely. This was unknown territory for her, and far too close to the concept of romantic love for comfort. It perhaps explained why already she'd had trouble keeping her physical feelings in check. The thought that she could become prey to such an unstable and potentially destructive state of mind sent her into a genuine panic. Falling in love was not part of her plans for her life, and she had no intention of doing it. Not now. Not ever!

She dragged in a deep breath and raised decidedly steely eyes. He was still looking at her, his food untouched on his lap, his expressive face betraying definite disappointment at her change of mood.

'I think,' she stated matter-of-factly, 'that once I've finished this I should get some sleep. I'm very tired.'

He gave her a long, unwavering look, then nodded. Slowly. Wryly.

'How soon will we have to be on our way in the morning?' she asked.

'I think we'll just play it by ear, don't you?' he said offhandedly.

This lackadaisical attitude went against her grain, for she had not achieved all she had achieved in life by playing things by ear. 'Can't you give me a time?' she demanded impatiently.

'After breakfast?' he suggested with a lazy grin.

'Oh, for heaven's sake!'

His smile faded to a pitying look. 'I think a few days' trekking in the desert will do you a world of good, Adrianna. You're far too uptight.'

'And you're far too sloppy,' she shot back. 'We can't all go through life on walkabout, you know.'

'Pity.'

She made an impatient sound, but underneath she was feeling a lot better for her outburst. She had been getting too cosy with Bryce for comfort. Maybe her lightweight feminine side was stirred by his macho body and laid-back charm, but that part of her brain which directed all her important decisions kept reminding her there was a lot about him she found downright irritating. He was domineering, chauvinistic, typically male. Not to mention lacking in ambition. Oh, she conceded, he seemed intelligent enough, but he obviously refused to use it. No way could she fall in love with someone like that. No way!

A wave of relief flooded through her. It was as though she had safely put him into a box, all packaged and labelled. *Bum*, it said. With a soothing sigh she began spooning the beans into her own mouth, only then realising how hungry she was. She started eating quite ravenously till Bryce stopped her with a question.

'Do you argue with your fiancé all the time?' he asked unexpectedly.

Startled, Adrianna blinked over at him, her fork hovering midway between her plate and her mouth. 'Of course not,' she retorted. 'Alan and I never argue.'

Bryce raised an eyebrow and lowered his own fork to his plate. '*What*? Lovers who don't squabble? Now that's an odd kind of love, I say.'

'Really?' She successfully captured a cool, faintly caustic tone, though behind the controlled mask she was being stirred up again. Who did this man think he was, questioning her relationship with Alan? 'I would have thought such a love had far more chance of lasting than one where people throw things at each other.'

And oddly enough, that was what she wanted to do all of a sudden, throw something at him. Her fingers fairly itched around the dinner plate. So much for having put him into a safe little box!

Bryce's face adopted an innocent pose. 'Whoever said anything about violence? I was merely saying that if there isn't any passion at the beginning of a relationship, then...' He broke off and shrugged carelessly.

'There's plenty of passion between Alan and me,' she lied fiercely.

Bryce forked a mouthful of food into his large mouth and sent a sceptical look her way. 'If you say so.'

She clenched her jaw in an effort to get control of herself, at the same time wanting quite desperately to lash out, to rant and rave at him, to even reach out and slap his smug, handsome face. Maybe then she could assuage that combination of needs which was bubbling up inside her—to both touch and hurt him.

With an enormous effort she copied one of his offhand shrugs. 'If you knew Alan then you wouldn't be making such ridiculous statements. He's the most handsome, charming, sexy man. Why, there must be hundreds of women who'd give anything to be in my shoes! Being asked to be Mrs Alan Carstairs is not a put-down, believe me!'

Adrianna was feeling so pleased with her little speech that it took some time before she realised Bryce was staring at her with eyes filled with true shock.

'Bryce... What is it? What did I say?'

'Mrs Alan Carstairs,' he repeated in a stunned voice. 'Alan Carstairs? Good God...'

'You...you *know* Alan?' Now she was the one who was shocked.

Bryce was shaking his head. 'If he's the same Alan Carstairs who lives at Vaucluse and owns all those Men About Town stores, then yes, I know him.'

'But...but how?' Adrianna gasped.

Bryce's glance was close to savage. 'Must you continually sound surprised over things about me? I'm not a total Philistine, dear lady. Neither have I spent my entire life in the nether regions. I lived in Sydney for a while when I was younger with relatives who were neighbours of your charming fiancé. In fact, I dated his secretary for a short time. Only he wasn't so charming in those days. He was an out-and-out bastard!'

Adrianna had to close her mouth before she could protest, but by this time Bryce was in full swing again.

'Oh, don't get me wrong,' he laughed mockingly. 'He wasn't a bastard with the ladies. From what I gathered, there *weren't* any ladies in his life. All he had time for was work, work, work, twenty-four hours a day, seven days a week. And heaven help any of his employees who didn't fancy doing the same!'

Adrianna found her voice at last. 'There's nothing wrong with being ambitious!'

'There certainly is,' Bryce retorted, 'if it's to the exclusion of everything else. My God, he didn't even take the day off to go to his father's funeral!'

'But that was at least ten years ago,' she defended hotly, though in reality she was shocked by Bryce's revelation. Even *she* had gone to her own father's funeral, and she doubted anyone had ever had less reason to.

'So it is,' Bryce admitted, the high colour in his face fading as he got control over his burst of temper. It was only then that Adrianna wondered why he had reacted so strongly to her news, anyway. What was it to him who she was marrying? In less than a week they would go their separate ways and never set eyes on each other again.

'I'm sure the Alan you knew has changed,' she stated categorically.

Those penetrating blue eyes gave her a slow once-over. 'Yes... I can see he must have.'

The implication shouldn't have annoyed her. But it did. 'Not that it's any of your business,' she pointed out coldly.

A muscle twitched along his jawline. 'No, I suppose it's not.'

'Then let's drop the subject, shall we?'

'By all means.'

A tense silence reigned as they both returned to finishing their meals, after which Bryce took her empty plate and began washing up in a plastic dish filled with billabong water.

'You should have let me do that,' Adrianna reproached.

His expression was totally unreadable as he turned his face her way. 'Why? Because it's traditionally women's work? I would have thought a liberated female like yourself would be pleased to see a man washing up.'

Her sigh was weary. 'I merely wanted to do something to help, and that was one thing you wouldn't be able to say I couldn't do as efficiently as you.'

'Well, it's done now,' came his curt answer, as he dried the last plate on a tea-towel and hung the damp cloth on the triangular iron construction that sat astride the fire.

The flames had by this time died down to hot embers, sending a golden glow over everything within a couple of metres. Bully lay sleeping in the sand a short distance away, his white flanks taking on an almost orange hue.

'Time for bed,' Bryce announced once he had tossed the dishwater away and put the empty tin with a stack of other equipment. He picked up the checked rug that had ended up lying in a heap at Adrianna's feet and began spreading it out on the sand near the dog. 'You can take my swag,' he told her. 'I'll sleep here.' He scooped the sand into a type of pillow beneath the blanket and stretched out, his hands coming up to rest behind his head, his eyes closing. He looked instantly as comfortable as though he were lying on the softest sofa.

Adrianna looked ruefully down at the rough sleeping bag she was sitting on. It consisted of two heavy blankets sewn together on three sides, with a rough-looking pillow attached. A queen-sized sleep-maker bed it was not! 'Er—I hate to disturb you, but could you get me my carry-all bag?' she asked, un-strapping her still damp leather sandals and putting them neatly beside the fire. 'I'd like to brush my hair before going to sleep. If I don't, it'll be impossible in the morning.'

He opened his eyes and looked at her as though such female attentions were totally unnecessary, given the situation, but fetched the bag as asked, and handed it over without a word of comment. She extracted the hairbrush and began to work her way through the mass of tangled knots, wondering idly what Bryce would say if he saw what she usually did before going to bed. It was like a royal ritual, the taking off her make-up with special remover, then the applying of various lotions and creams to the different parts of her face and body. Not that she was obsessed by her looks, but she was sensible enough to know that a well-groomed and attractive appearance was important in the business world.

She stopped brushing for a moment and ran her fingertips over her forehead and cheeks. Her skin felt very dehydrated and her lips were rough and dry. Another day of this and they'd crack right open.

'You look fine,' Bryce startled her by saying sharply.

She glanced over to where he was watching her from the checked blanket. 'My lips are terribly dry. Heaven knows what they'll be like after five more days of this!'

'I have some cream you could use on them,' he volunteered, much to her surprise, and promptly got up once again, striding over to search through one of his many canvas packs. He returned with a small white tube in one hand.

'What is it?' she asked as he dropped to his knees next to her, unscrewed the cap and squeezed a dob on to his first two fingers of his right hand.

'Lanolin.'

'I ... I can do that,' she choked out when he went to spread it on her lips himself.

'You'll get your fingers sticky if you do. It's no trouble.'

Adrianna literally held her breath as his creamed fingers made contact with her mouth. It was all she could do not to suck in a gasping breath when he began rubbing and massaging the cream into her lips with slow, circular motions. As it was, her stomach twisted into knots and she started mentally counting to ten, assuring herself that by then it would be over.

But the ten seconds came and went and still the erotic torture went on and on. Just as she was sure he was finished his fingertips returned to dab lightly at her top lip, then the lower, then deep into the corners, after which he began moving them round and round her mouth as though tracing a circle. She felt the blood race to her lips, making them swell and tingle.

'Haven't you finished?' she said at last in a strangled voice. Her eyes were beginning to feel oddly heavy and she looked up through half-closed lashes at his.

His returning look was equally heavy-lidded, and she knew then, knew with a startling stab of shock deep inside her, that he was deliberately prolonging doing what he was doing, was indeed becoming as turned on by it as she was.

'I think that's enough,' she said breathlessly.

His gaze dropped to her parted lips, then lifted back to her eyes. 'No,' he said in a voice thick with arousal. 'No, Adrianna . . . It's not nearly enough . . .'

Any desire she was secretly harbouring was swamped by panic in the face of his fierce and passionate resolve. It tore deep, warning her that if she let him make love to her he would take far more than her body. 'Bryce, no!' she rasped.

He ignored her feeble protest, a single fingertip returning to trace her mouth again, more slowly this time, very seductively, his eyes glazing as they followed its sensual path. A tiny moan whimpered deep in her throat, her stunned and terrified mind fighting a desperate battle with the temptation to part her quivering lips even wider, to suck his flesh into her mouth.

She struck his hand away with a sob and jerked her head back. 'I said *no*!' she cried.

The almost incoherent expression on his face cleared as he focused on her wide eyes. 'You want me to,' he said, so calmly that it was doubly shocking.

She gaped at him. 'I don't!'

'Yes, you do,' he repeated. 'You want me to make love to you. Here... Now...'

For a few horrified seconds she just stared at him, drugged by the sensual power of his deep, sexy voice. But then she was shaking her head—wildly, frantically. 'That's not true!' she cried.

Her denial seemed to galvinise him into action. He grabbed her by the shoulders and shook her. 'Yes, it is! Why don't you admit it, damn you? It's there... between us... has been all day. That's why we've ended up sniping at each other tonight. It's called desire, Adrianna. Desire... Stop being such a little hypocrite and admit it!' His eyes were challenging, taunting. Arrogantly certain.

Something exploded in her head, something equally forceful and certain. No man pushed her into a corner, either emotionally or physically. No man! 'All *right*!' she screamed at him. 'All *right*! I want you to make love to me! OK?'

She yanked away from him and stood up, throwing her hands in the air in an angry, dismissive gesture. 'Does that make you happy? Does it boost your insufferably large male ego to know you attract me against all the dictates of common sense and decency?'

She glared down at him with blisteringly cold eyes. 'Because I don't *want* to want you, Bryce McLean. Even if I wasn't committed to someone else, your sort of man is not for me, not even for a one-night stand! You country cowboys have no real respect for women.

Oh, sure, you like them in your bed every now and then, but that's where it ends. Then it's back to your animals and your mates and your drinking binges down at the pub. Believe me, I've seen your type in action. So just *wanting* you is as far as I intend going. I have no intention of putting that want into action, of letting you use this unfortunate weakness of mine to satisfy your own animalistic urges. And please, for pity's sake don't have the gall to call it making love! With you it would only be having sex, nothing more. Men like you know as much about love as Dumbo there knows about *whoa*! At least Alan knows how to treat a woman. Oh, yes, sneer all you like, but he makes love like a dream and I care for him dearly, and I wouldn't dream of being unfaithful to him.'

Those blue eyes blazed up at her with an anger that looked like outstripping hers. He slowly got to his feet, looming over her like an avenging angel. Only this angel was straight out of hell, all fire and brimstone and dark menace. Adrianna backed away from him, but he followed, pulling her to a shaking halt with an iron grip on her upper arms.

'Bulldust!' he snarled down into her wide grey eyes. 'You don't love Carstairs—no woman could love that cold computer of a man. At least, not the woman I've seen you to be. You're an intelligent, proud, spirited lady, Adrianna. You couldn't give your heart, your soul, to a man like that!'

His mouth twisted into an ugly grimace. 'I'm not saying you haven't given him your body, or that he wouldn't know how to push the right buttons. He probably had all the correct moves programmed into his silicon chip brain the second he passed puberty. But Adrianna . . .'

He yanked her against him, his fierce embrace punching the breath from her lungs. His hands dropped to cup her buttocks, lifting and kneading them before using his bruising hold to pull her breathtakingly close. 'If *I* made love to you,' he promised huskily, 'you'd know the difference. Say what you will about the sort of man you think I am, but at least I am that—a *man*, not a sleek-suited masquerade who's more concerned with his perfectly orchestrated technique than the woman he's with. My God, when I take you, my hot-blooded harridan, you'll *know* you've been taken, I can assure you!'

A moan escaped her lips as he pressed her even closer, moulding her soft stomach around the evidence of his claim. She tried to fight the hot tide of desire that washed up through her, her stunned mind hardly believing what was happening to her. It was a nightmare all right. Not the nightmare she had thought this trip would be, but a nightmare all the same. This man was making her forget everything she had just said. Her lifelong resolutions . . . her opinion of him . . . Alan . . . Everything!

All she wanted was to lose herself in the orgy of sensuality that was invading every pore of her body. It had already taken over her imagination, evoking startlingly clear fantasies to further tantalise her senses. Herself and Bryce naked; his doing incredible things to her; and herself, doing all the things she had never done or ever really wanted to do with a man.

Her pulse-rate took off and the blood began to pound in her veins, her temples, her head.

With a weird sense of fate closing in she tipped her head back and lifted her chin in readiness for the possession of his mouth. He stared down at her, blue eyes smouldering like hot ice. Her lips parted. Not just for him to kiss them but to offer her total capitulation in the plainest, most shocking words. 'Bryce...'

But no sooner had his name left her lips than a memory, stark and vivid, leapt into her brain. That of a woman, sitting at a battered kitchen table, her head in her hands, crying, saying she was pregnant—*again*—letting out all her despair and misery to the only person who would listen. Her ten-year-old daughter. And the daughter, unhappy, helpless, wondering why her mother kept making babies with a man who didn't give a hoot about her or his never-ending brood, who didn't support them, didn't love them, didn't even bother to come home most nights. But all the woman could say was that she loved him.

The memory burnt a path into Adrianna's brain, obliterating her desire as swiftly as a winter storm destroys the last remnants of autumn. Fear swept in instead, a fear that made her strike out blindly.

She lifted her knee and rammed it upwards between Bryce's thighs, then staggered backwards to watch, wide-eyed, as pain destroyed his arousal as effectively as the past had destroyed hers. He doubled over in sheer agony, his hands clutching his groin, his sharp inward breath more revealing than the loudest moan.

But when his eyes lifted to hers, his pain-filled, bewildered, accusing eyes, Adrianna was immediately consumed with an overwhelming remorse. 'Oh, Bryce!' she cried piteously, and stumbled forward to try to help him.

He repelled her with a vicious glance.

Bully, woken by the incident, came to his master's side and whimpered. With a grimace Bryce bent down and lightly touched the dog's ear. 'I'll be OK in a minute, boy,' he muttered between tightly drawn lips. 'Don't worry.'

Tears welled up into Adrianna's eyes. 'Oh, Bryce, I'm so sorry...'

'So am I,' he groaned.

'I didn't realise...'

'God!'

'Please forgive me.'

'Not bloody likely!'

She blinked. 'Oh...' She wasn't used to having an apology thrown back in her face.

He was finally able to straighten, though he was obviously still hurting. 'Don't look so petrified,' he grated through clenched teeth. 'I have more respect for my private parts than to come near you again. God...' He dragged in another deep sigh and let it out raggedly.

'Oh, Bryce, I... I...'

'For Pete's sake, don't you have any idea when to shut up, woman? Go to bed!'

She scrambled into the rough sleeping bag and just lay there, a shattered emotional wreck. One part of her kept saying she had done the right thing, the only thing. But still...

Eventually she risked a glimpse over at where Bryce was still standing, staring across at her, a black look of deep puzzlement on his face.

'What... what is it?' she asked nervously.

Bryce didn't answer her question, giving her a dismissive shrug and turning his back on her, leaving Adrianna with the impression that he would like to turn his back on her in more ways than one.

Not that she blamed him. No doubt he was now bitterly regretting his noble action in going to rescue her. He was probably wishing that he'd never set eyes on her, or that he had left her to the mercy of the desert.

Adrianna's mind whirled on and on, making her toss and turn in the rough bed. But finally sleep stole across her troubled soul, bringing with it a soothing blanket of oblivion. It was just as well, perhaps, that Adrianna couldn't see what the morrow would bring. Otherwise she might not have slept at all.

CHAPTER FIVE

ADRIANNA was dragged from a deep sleep quite abruptly, her eyelids propelled open by a cacophony of raucous birdcalls. She blinked volubly at the stark brightness of daylight before staring upwards into the towering pink branches of the river-gums under which Bryce had made his camp.

A flock of black cockatoos, their flamboyant orange tail-feathers flashing in the morning light, were jumping from branch to branch and screeching their strident music. Adrianna put her hands over her ears, but continued to watch them, awed by the birds' undeniable beauty. Large and glossy, they had a proud carriage and a wild, wicked beauty, looking like winged devils as they darted this way and that, their ebony coats the colour of Hades, their flaming tails a glimpse of hell-fire. All in all, magnificent, breathtaking.

But the *noise* they made! Adrianna rolled to one side, closing her eyes against the glare, and it was then that the memory of what had happened the night before finally filtered in.

Oh God! she groaned silently, and closed her eyes even tighter.

Thank the lord her back was to Bryce's bed! She couldn't look at him, couldn't face him. The reality that there were still five days of his sole companionship to go loomed large and fearful in her mind.

It wasn't that she didn't trust him. If he'd been going to do anything to her, he would have last night, when his blood and temper were up. But he hadn't. In fact, he'd shown an astounding amount of restraint, considering. Some men would have struck back at her quite violently.

It was herself she didn't trust. Or at least, that part of herself she seemed unable to control where Bryce was concerned. She still couldn't believe the intensity of her physical reaction to him. Though at least now she doubted if he would continue in that light, almost flirtatious manner he adopted sometimes. Neither, she suspected, would he be smiling and joking all the time.

This would provide her with some relief, she decided with a sigh. A few scowls and frowns were infinitely preferable to the way his eyes lit up so attractively whenever that irrepressible grin split his handsome face. Yes... If he kept his distance and treated her with cold wariness, or even downright contempt, perhaps she would survive this nightmare.

Perhaps...

It was an infinitely depressing realisation that if she hadn't had that vivid memory of her mother's misery she'd have let Bryce make love to her. By now he would have left her bare of more than her clothes. He would have also stripped her of her pride and self-respect, as her father had stripped her mother. What that man had done to that poor sweet woman didn't bear thinking about!

At least her mother's life now was a lot easier and happier, Adrianna reassured herself. The generous cheque she sent every month allowed her to rent a nice place with plenty left over for herself. Of course she probably gave some of it to those rotten ungrateful sons of hers, but there wasn't much Adrianna could do about that. She could hardly put conditions on the money. But by God, she wouldn't voluntarily

give those brothers of hers a cent. Not a single cent!
They were as lazy and useless and selfish as her father
had been.

A deep sigh wafted from Adrianna's lips. She didn't
want to think about her family, didn't want to think
of all those years she had spent, having to come home
from school and do everything most mothers would
normally have already done. Except that *her* mother
had had to go out and work long hours as a cleaner
to bring *some* money in to feed and clothe their ever-
expanding family. Adrianna had two older brothers
and five younger ones before her mother stopped
getting pregnant.

In Adrianna's view it would have been fair if all
the children had bogged in and helped around the
house—not to mention her perennially unemployed
father—but because she was a girl, and her father was
the chauvinist to beat all chauvinists, it had fallen to
her alone to do all the housework and cooking and
minding of the younger ones.

Adrianna's teenage years had gone by in an endless
round of dirty nappies and screaming kids and never-
ending baby-sitting. There had been moments when
she had wanted to wring her baby brothers' necks—
literally—her feelings sometimes so violent and re-
sentful that even now she could not remember them
without feeling guilty. Obviously she wasn't the self-
sacrificing maternal type.

Though it seemed unfair to condemn herself too
strongly after what she had had to put up with. But
either way, the thought of having a husband who
expected her to stay home and have baby after baby
sent shivers up and down her spine.

Which brought her to another mind-blowing
thought where Bryce was concerned. Last night,

before she'd woken up to herself, she hadn't given a single thought to pregnancy! It just showed you how irrational a female could get when her hormones were working overtime.

Quite automatically her mind started ticking over dates. It was mildly consoling to realise that she was unlikely to conceive at this time of the month. What wasn't so consoling was that she still thought she might need this reassurance. It was as though, down deep, she believed she might still encourage Bryce to make love to her, which was so self-destructive she had to be crazy.

What about Alan? she berated herself. Don't you have any loyalty to him?

Not enough, apparently, to ward off this over-whelming desire. Which upset Adrianna consider-ably. For she was by nature a loyal and true person, and Alan was not at all the unfeeling bastard Bryce had tried to paint him to be last night. He might be hardworking and ambitious, but underneath he was a good man. And he *did* put aside time for things other than work these days.

There was his relationship with her, for instance, and just recently she had found out that he had a ward he was responsible for, the young daughter of good friends of his who'd drowned in a ferry accident three years previously. Adrianna had seen her photo in his wallet and asked him about her.

Apparently the girl had been fifteen and in a boarding school when the tragedy had happened and he had been named as executor in her parents' will. Ebony was her name—Ebony Theroux. It seemed Alan visited her occasionally at the boarding school, taking her parents' roles at speech nights and concerts and such. The girl also came to his home during her holidays, where she was a warm favourite with his widowed mother. She would live there permanently, it appeared, after she left school at the end of the year.

Thinking of Alan's home brought another thought to Adrianna's mind. Where, she wondered, would she and Alan live after they were married? Surely not with his mother and his young ward...

A frown puckered her brow as she lay there, chewing away on her thoughts, and gradually she became aware that everything was very quiet around her. She peeped a look over her shoulder and upwards, and saw that the cockatoos had left. The silky green leaves were still and silent, not even a breeze rustling through them. But it surprised her that Bryce wasn't up yet, poking around, rattling the billy or loading up the camels. And what about Bully? Shouldn't she have heard a bark or two?

Apprehension struck fast and furious and she was instantly on the move, rolling over and jerking upright as if a bomb had gone off at her feet. Her eyes darted here, there, everywhere!

Bryce's blanket was coldly empty. There were no camels grazing in the lush surrounds of the billabong. And Bully, like his master, was nowhere in sight.

Shock was a sick turning over in her stomach. He's gone and left me, she thought. Left me to die...

But then her brain clicked fully into gear. She saw that all his packs were still here, piled up nearby. Even his hat. Surely he would have taken his *hat* if he didn't mean to come back? She searched for some reason for his absence. Perhaps he was out for an early morning ride!

The idea seemed ludicrous to Adrianna that anyone would ride camels for pleasure as though they were

horses. But she clung to the notion, for she could think
of nothing else. And if she didn't have some expla-
nation—however stupid—to soothe her growing fears,
she would have gone mad.

The silent empty minutes ticked away as she waited
for Bryce to reappear. After half an hour, she busied
herself finding some firewood from under the trees
and getting the campfire going again, the dry dead
branches catching alight quickly from the still glowing
embers. She even boiled a billy, found some tea-bags
and made herself some tea.

But that was as far as she went, her agitation making
her continually walk out to where the green grass finished and the sands began. Shading her eyes with her
hands, she scanned the distant dunes, willing Bryce
to suddenly appear.

He didn't.

After nearly an hour of this torturous waiting, she
slumped down next to the campfire and dissolved into
tears. And it was while she was crying that she heard
the most wonderful sound she had ever heard—
Jumbo's cowbell.

Her relief was like a huge tidal wave, washing
through her, her tears instantly dry, adrenalin firing
her veins with life-giving energy. Ignoring the still
protesting stiffness in her muscles, she jumped up and
ran towards the sound, her fair hair flying out behind
her, her feet unshod, a joyous smile breaking over her
face.

She was halfway to the sandhills when she spied
them, coming over the crest, Bryce on foot, leading
the camels, Bully padding along beside him, tongue
lolling out of the side of his mouth. If Adrianna had
been approaching more slowly and with any degree
of observation, she would have seen that Bryce looked

tired and disgruntled, his appearance unkempt with bloodshot eyes and a beard-roughened chin. He was hardly in a receptive mood for the way she flew at him, throwing her arms madly around his neck.

'Oh, Bryce, Bryce, thank heaven!' she cried, her chest heaving against his. 'I was so worried. I . . .'

She froze when she saw the look in his eyes. It would have killed a cobra at ten feet. Before she could react, he dropped the reins, lifted his hands, grabbed her wrists and unpeeled her arms from his neck, depositing them back by her side and pushing her aside as though she were a contaminated person who had broken quarantine. 'Do you *mind*?' he said in a voice dipped in lemon.

Adrianna now felt sick in a totally different way. She had thought she would welcome his contempt, his coldness. But the reality was far, far different. Something shrivelled up inside her, making her want to crumple up and burst into tears again. She longed for one of his smiles, one of his light remarks. Even a casual civility would be better than this ghastly scorn.

'I would have thought you'd have a bit more sense, Adrianna,' he bit out with another savage look, 'than to throw your bra-less breasts against me like that. I would appreciate it if you would keep your distance, in future. And perhaps your jacket on? That way I might get out of this desert intact!'

Her cheeks flushed bright with guilt and shame. And indignation. She was perfectly decently dressed, if a little crumpled. 'I wasn't throwing myself at you in that way,' she argued, tossing her hair back from her face in a defiant gesture. 'I was just so happy and relieved to see you. Surely you must realise how worried I was when I woke to find you and the camels gone?'

His eyebrows lifted as he realised what she must have thought. 'Am I so low in your opinion that you believed I would resort to murder?'

She couldn't think what to say to that.

'Not that you don't *deserve* murdering,' he added testily.

Again she said nothing.

'Not very communicative this morning, are we?' he went on. 'What a pleasant change!' He picked up the reins and brushed past her, striding back towards the camp.

Adrianna ran after him till she was level with his shoulder. 'Where...where *were* you?' she asked breathlessly.

'Finding the rotten damned camels, of course! The mongrels took off in the night.'

'But you said they were tame!'

'Not *that* tame,' he snapped, then added in a dark mutter, 'I should have hobbled them before I went to bed. I usually do.'

'Then why didn't you?' she asked. Hobbling must mean tying up or staking out, she frowned to herself.

His sideways glance was blistering. 'I had other things on my mind!'

She bit her bottom lip.

'Besides,' he growled, 'I didn't really think they'd wander, with all that lush feed and water virtually at their feet. Perhaps that mad bull came back skulking around in the night and spooked them. The stupid fools were heading back for the salt-pan when I found them. If it hadn't been for Bully, I wouldn't have even considered looking that way.'

'Thank heaven for Bully, then,' she put in.

'You're not wrong there. I wouldn't like to walk my way from here, I can tell you. And speaking of walking, I think, Adrianna,' Bryce pointed out curtly, 'that you'd be advised to wear your sandals. That is if you want those delicate little feet of yours to last the distance.'

Despite the sarcasm in Bryce's voice, Adrianna detected a reluctant compliment in his words. She glanced down at her feet, acknowledging that she *did* have attractively dainty feet, with small slender toes and nicely shaped toenails. Yet Alan had never remarked on them, or even noticed them, for that matter. A shiver of pleasure rippled over her skin that Bryce was still so aware of her.

There quickly followed a black wave of self-disgust. All that self-lecturing and I'm no closer to controlling my feelings for this man, she thought. Even with his obvious derision, I'm looking for signs that he still fancies me. Because the truth is, I want him to still fancy me, I want him to fancy me so damned much that he'll somehow ignore what happened last night. I want him to use his male strength and natural sexual aggression to force me to admit these underlying feelings, to force me to... to what?

The possibilities made her throat go dry, made her heart pound madly within her breast.

She slanted him a quick sideways glance, glimpsing the stubborn set of his jaw as he marched along, a hint of suppressed violence in the way his lips were pressed together in a thin line. Perhaps she should be grateful for his hostility towards her, she thought bleakly. It might be the best protection she would ever have. She certainly couldn't rely on her own self-restraint!

They reached the camp, where Bryce led the camels over to give them a drink of water while he held the reins, leaving Adrianna standing beside the fire like a shag on a rock. She decided to get Bryce a cup of tea whether he wanted her to or not, carrying it over to him. He was clearly startled as she pressed it into his hand, his eyes betraying a reluctant flash of pleasure. But it was quickly gone as a stony expression took its place. 'Thanks,' he muttered, and lifted the mug to drink.

'I... I'd make you some breakfast too,' she said, 'but I don't know what supplies are in what bag. If you'd just show me...' Her voice broke off when he made some scowling sound and she sighed. 'Please, Bryce... I said I was sorry... Can't we forget about last night?'

His glance was long and hard. 'Can *you*?'

She stiffened. 'I'd like to try.'

Bryce gave a tired, mocking laugh.

'OK, so you hate me now,' she said softly. 'Fair enough. But we're stuck with each other for a while yet and it's far better all round if we try to get along, at least on the surface. Don't you agree?'

His eyes were fixed on her face, narrowed unreadable eyes. Oh, how she wished she knew what he was thinking!

'Very well,' he said curtly. 'I'm not an unreasonable man.'

Adrianna smiled with relief, but the smile faded quickly when his face tightened at the sight of it. Clearly their truce was not supposed to extend to smiles. And if she were honest with herself, Adrianna knew that was a good idea. Smiles were hardly the way to keep a man at bay. Or a woman, for that matter.

'One thing especially,' she went on in a more matter-of-fact voice. 'I'd like to help more, Bryce. I'm not stupid, really I'm not.'

There was the faintest twitch at the corner of his grim mouth. 'All right.'

He was as good as his word. First of all, he showed her all his supplies, which were extensive, even including a battery-operated razor which quickly returned his stubbly chin to its former clean-shaven state, after which they breakfasted on tinned peaches and muesli, topped with reconstituted powdered milk. More tea followed, then an apple each. Then he gave her some basic chores to do like washing up, filling the water bags and covering the fire with sand while he packed and loaded the camels, sharing the load between Dumbo and Jumbo.

One thing she noticed, though, was Bryce's reluctance to look straight at her, or touch her in any way. There was certainly no hint of his offering to apply either the sunscreen or insect repellent he gave her. Even their accidental brushing against each other resulted in his either moving himself further away, or actually flinching. Adrianna thought he was overdoing it a bit, and in the end she said so, which brought a ghost of a smile to his lips.

'Better to be safe than sorry, I say,' was his answering remark.

But he was a fraction more relaxed after that, and actually touched her thigh while getting her saddled up without looking as if he'd encountered a leper. Adrianna wasn't sure what to think about his behaviour. She couldn't believe he was actually afraid of her assaulting him. Which left a possibility that she found both disturbing and tantalising at the same time. He might hate her, but he also might still desire her. Far too much, obviously, for his peace of mind...

Two hours after Bryce's return they were on their way. By noon they had covered several miles, moving along at a steady walk, following the path of a dry creek bed which Bryce said had intermittent water-holes. He was right, and they rested at one for nearly two hours over lunch, but encountered nothing that day as large and lovely as the lagoon they'd just left. Nevertheless, it was a far pleasanter route to travel along than the desert and dunes, shade from the river-gums providing a cooling respite from the fierce heat. It was great too that the flies no longer bothered her. In fact, by late in the afternoon, although tired, Adrianna felt quite relaxed.

Bryce was right about the desert, she thought. It had a way of emptying one's mind—a bit like flying. It also played tricks with time. Several times she thought an hour had passed, but then she'd find out only several minutes had gone by. This effect, com-bined with the drugging heat, meant that one's whole being was lulled into a type of drowsy trance which was oddly soothing. Her body soon learnt to move with the rock and sway of the camel without tension, without strain, and as they ambled along late in the afternoon her eyelids grew heavier, and heavier, and heavier...

'You're not going to sleep sitting up, are you?'

Her eyes shot open to see Bryce alongside her. Dumbo, she noticed with a jolt, had stopped walking.

She blinked. 'You know what? I think I was,' she said, surprise in her voice.

Bryce laughed.

A warmth rushed into Adrianna's heart. It was good to hear him laugh again. And she smiled at him.

Immediately his laughter stopped and he jerked his head away. 'We'll camp here for the night,' he announced abruptly. 'This is as good a waterhole as we're going to get along this part of the journey.'

'Oh...' She looked at the small, slightly muddy pond in front of them, trying valiantly not to let his return to sharpness bother her.

'Well? Are you going to sit there dreaming all day?' Bryce asked impatiently. 'You said you wanted to help!'

'Oh yes... yes...' She gave him a flustered glance, but he was already looking away from her.

The evening passed eventually, but not pleasantly. Bryce did a good imitation of a sulky Marlon Brando, only opening his lips to mutter some instruction to her, or growl at Bully, who seemed to have the devil in him and was taking pleasure in antagonising the camels. After a severe scolding the dog skulked over and sat next to Adrianna, something he hadn't done before. But when she stretched her hand out to pat him he snapped at it.

Like master, like dog, she thought ruefully.

The ground wasn't as soft as the sand around the lagoon either, but when she mentioned this fact Bryce gave her a scathing look.

'Must you complain all the time?' he growled. 'This isn't the Ritz, you know.'

'But I don't complain all the time,' she defended, stung by his accusation. 'I... Oh, to *hell* with you, Bryce McLean!' she snapped suddenly. 'Just because you're in a filthy mood don't think you can take it out on me. I'm not a *dog*, you know!'

'No,' he flung back at her, 'you're a silly damned bitch!'

Silence fell over them like a sodden blanket. Bryce made another scowling noise and stalked off into the night.

Adrianna had never felt so hurt in all her life.

Tears sprang to her eyes and she threw herself down on the bedroll, burying her face in the lumpy pillow and sobbing noisily.

In typical female fashion she half expected him to hear her, to return and comfort her. But he didn't, leaving her to her misery and bewilderment. She found it both disconcerting and perplexing that the worse he treated her, the more she wanted him. It was crazy in the extreme, and very distressing, mostly because it went against all that she considered both logical and normal. Shouldn't a woman be attracted to gentleness and kindness and consideration, not macho displays of rudeness and total disregard for her feelings?

She took a long time to get to sleep, a long, long time. Long enough to decide that she was a damned fool, that Bryce was a nasty bit of goods and that she would never speak to him again as long as she lived!

It was a resolution that lasted till morning. After all, it was hard not to speak to the man after he'd saved her life.

CHAPTER SIX

She was lying on her back when she woke slowly the next morning just before the dawn, and became gradually aware of an unnatural weight on the blanket, across her thighs. Could it be Bully? was her first thought. Probably, she decided.

Yet somehow she couldn't bring herself to take a look and tiny shivers kept running up and down her spine. The reasoning behind her nervous reaction finally slotted into her sleep-slowed brain. The weight wasn't heavy enough for such a solid, nuggety dog...

In that case, what was it?

Her breathing began coming in short, shallow pants as she tried to gather up the courage to look. Slowly she started to lift her head from the pillow, her heart hammering painfully against her ribs.

'Don't move,' came the low, husky warning form the direction of Bryce's blanket.

Her heart jumped into her throat, but she lowered her head with excruciating slowness back down again. 'What is it?' she rasped back, not daring to even twist her head to one side so that she could see where Bryce was.

'Just...don't...move,' he repeated, each word low and emphasised.

'Oh, God...'

There was only thing it could be, of course. A snake. A *big* snake, by the feel of it.

Adrianna abhorred snakes. Even a picture of a snake made her skin crawl. The thought that one was lying in her lap, with only a blanket between its deadly fangs and herself, made her feel ill. Perspiration broke out on her forehead as the seconds ticked away.

'Where are you? What are you going to do?' she whispered urgently.

'Will you shut up?' hissed Bryce, his voice this time coming from nearby.

She could see him now, crouching near her head, bending over her. Slowly, ever so slowly, he slid his hands under her armpits and took a firm grip on her upper body. 'On the count of three,' he told her quietly and steadily, 'I'm going to yank you out. OK?'

'OK,' she agreed, terrified.

'One ... two ... *three*!'

She shot out of the rough sleeping bag like a cannonball out of a cannon, her whole body landing on Bryce's with a resounding thud. But he was instantly rolling away from under her, snatching up his rifle and firing. Whatever had been on that blanket was now sorry it chose that place to sleep, Adrianna thought dazedly.

When Bryce returned to gather her body up into his arms she began to shake. 'What ... what kind of snake was it?' she asked.

He held her away from him briefly and gave her a wry smile. 'And how did you know it was a snake, Miss Smarty-pants?'

'You're ... you're not the only one who can make a l-logical con-conclusion. Bryce ... why am I sh-shaking so?'

'Shock. You'll be all right in a little while. Want to look at the body?'

A shudder reverberated through her as she glanced reluctantly down at the huge, ugly mass of reptilian remains.

'Just as well Bully's off chasing an early morning rabbit,' he told her, 'or he'd have dived on this fellow for sure, and God knows what would have happened then. It was a King Brown,' he added. 'Deadly as hell.'

Adrianna went weak at the knees, but Bryce propped her up again. 'I think what you need is a slug of brandy,' he said, then led her over and settled her on the log. She slumped down like a sack of potatoes.

Bryce squeezed her shoulder before walking over to the supplies. 'I have a medicinal quantity here somewhere...' He rummaged through one of his personal bags. 'Ah, here it is.' And he produced a small flask.

He came back, unscrewing the cap on the way, and handing it over without a glass. 'Just take a swig,' he suggested. 'I'll risk your germs.'

She did as she was told, coughing slightly as she swallowed too much too quickly. 'You're always getting me reviving drinks,' she said.

'You're always needing them,' he chuckled, taking the flask from her and rescrewing the lid.

She smiled up at him. 'True... But I can't help it if my body's not immune to all these dramas the way yours is.'

His face darkened, and she wondered what she had said or done wrong now. What Adrianna hadn't realised was that when she had smiled up at Bryce her eyes had sparkled flirtatiously as a woman's did when she was as aware of a man as she was of him. It wasn't a deliberate thing, her throwing out of a sexual challenge, but it was there all the same.

'My body isn't immune to anything,' he said coldly, 'as I'm sure you are well aware. It's as vulnerable and mortal as the next man's.'

There was no hiding the surprise in her eyes at his about-turn, and he shook his head in exasperation. 'I wish you'd make up your mind,' he went on irritably, 'what you want of me.'

'Want of you?' she repeated blankly, stunned by the swift change in both his mood and the situation. Suddenly all was tense and electric between them.

'Look, I'm not going to beat around the bush any longer,' Bryce ground out. 'I'm not into playing the sophisticated sexual games you city folk indulge in. I call a spade a spade and to hell with it! I want you, Adrianna. I've wanted you from the first second I laid eyes on you, running towards me.'

Adrianna gaped. He'd wanted her all along? But he'd given her no indication. No indication at all! Not till the lagoon...

'I didn't think it was the right time or place to come on strong straight away,' Bryce continued. 'And then you dropped your bombshell about being engaged. Damn it, I thought. She's out of bounds. OK, laugh it off. Make light of it. It's nothing anyway but a physical thing. An ache, like a headache. Take a cold swim every night. But then all of a sudden, the status quo changed. You wanted me back. I saw it, in your eyes, in the lagoon. Then, to top it all off, I found out that the man you were engaged to wasn't worth spitting on! I figured there wasn't any reason why I shouldn't go after you, no reason why I shouldn't just do what your eyes kept telling me you wanted of me. So when the opportunity presented itself—with the lip cream—I began taking it. With unfortunate and rather painful results, however.'

'Bryce, I...'

'Be quiet and hear me out!'

Her mouth snapped shut.

'I know you said you were sorry,' he bit out. 'But that doesn't wash away your reasons for suddenly going cold on me last night and almost damaging me for life! Don't think I don't know why you did it, because I *do*! And lady, I don't take kindly to that sort of thing. Not kindly at all!'

He glared at her with bitter resentment which only increased her confusion. How could he possibly know about her background, about her sudden vision of her mother?

'Don't bother putting that innocently bewildered look into those beautiful grey eyes of yours, Adrianna. You're about as innocent as a politician! You and I know exactly why you got cold feet last night. At the last moment you couldn't lower yourself to actually let a man like me put his grubby hands on you, could you? You don't think I'm good enough for you, which is why now, no matter what you say or do, no matter how often you go hot and cold, I have no intention of touching you.'

He set wintry eyes on her wide-eyed face. 'You judged me, madam, without even knowing me. You slotted me into the ne'er-do-well category and closed the file! But that's all right, because I'm returning you the favour. I'm slotting you into the category of snobbish, mercenary career bitch who wants her cake and wants to eat it too; a super-suave millionaire to satisfy her need for money and social position, and a bit of rough stuff on the side to satisfy her libido. How am I going? Am I close? After all, you *have* finally got over your qualms at dirtying your hands, haven't you?' His laughter grated over her nerves like chalk on a blackboard. 'That's why you're being nice to me all of a sudden, isn't it?'

He flung this last derisive remark at her, a taunting glint in his eyes that demanded a reaction. It brought a reaction all right, but one she didn't give him the satisfaction of seeing. The half-truths behind what he'd just said evoked undermining elements of guilt and shame, but this last accusation was so patently false and unjust, so cruel and nasty, that she refused to concede anything to him.

Adrianna squared her shoulders and lifted her chin, her eyes almost as chilling as his as they flashed across the space between them. 'I would say your skill with a rifle is far more accurate than your assessment of me and my motives,' she grated, her words like chipped ice. 'As I said once before, Bryce, I was briefly—*very* briefly—attracted to you. Please put it down to an aberration after the plane crash, a re-action to the gratitude I felt for your Lawrence of Arabia rescue. I was quickly over it. It seems to me that you must have an over-inflated opinion of your sex appeal if you think that every woman who's pleasant to you wants to rip your clothes off. There again, perhaps you judge everyone else by your own urges, which seem to quickly get out of hand. After all, you've just confessed to desiring a woman you dislike. I find that a contradiction in terms. I know I certainly couldn't continue to desire a man I disliked.'

Her shrug was most convincingly indifferent. 'Anyway, it's a comfort to know that you'll play at being a gentleman for the rest of the trip, though may I suggest, by way of precaution, that you keep having a cold swim every night!'

Her words shocked him, she could see. Or was it her manner—her confident, commanding, coldly caustic manner? Little did he know that inside she was weeping, weeping for the messed-up future that lay ahead of her. For how could she marry Alan now? How could she go into his bed every night, wishing he were someone else...

'My God,' Bryce muttered, his bottom lip curling over in disgust. 'You're more of a bitch than I thought!'

Adrianna closed her heart to his derision. 'Think what you like. The fact of the matter is that all this will be irrelevant in a few days' time. We won't ever see each other again. So let's try to be civil, shall we? Or is that too much to ask for a macho outback man like you?'

Adrianna knew straight away that she shouldn't have used such a goading, inflammatory tone. But it was too late now to take it all back. He would only scorn any attempt at an apology.

A smile slowly came to Bryce's mouth, a wickedly cruel smile that struck dread into her soul. 'You'd be surprised how civilised I can be, Adrianna,' he said in a voice like silk. Or was it like a snake?

Apprehension rippled over the surface of her skin. If he dared touch her she would have him arrested for rape! 'I'm glad to hear it,' she said, her throat clamping tight in an effort to control her shaking voice. It made her words come out curtly, as though coated with contempt. 'Now, do you think we could get on with things? Perhaps if we can make really good time we might be back to that cattle station of yours in two days instead of three.'

'Cattle station of mine?' he repeated archly.

'You know what I mean... The place where you work. Dover Downs or whatever it's called.'

'Ah yes, Dover Downs, the place where I work... Well, if you're prepared to spend long hours in the saddle I think we might manage it in two days, if that's what you really want.'

'That's what I want,' she said stiffly.

'Be it on your own head,' he muttered.

It wasn't just on her head. It was also on her bottom, her poor stiff, aching bottom. Not to mention the rest of her. But by heaven they covered some ground that day, the camels barely able to pick up their feet when they were still being pushed along the creek bed as the sun finally set. 'Bryce,' she said at last, her voice quavering with exhaustion, 'I can't go on. I . . .'

'Can't go on?' he scoffed. 'Why not? It was what you wanted, wasn't it?'

'Because . . . because . . .' In the end she didn't have to give him a reason, for she slithered sideways off the saddle and on to the sandy ground in a dead faint.

When she came to, it was cold, the sky was pitch dark and she was in the bedroll. Bryce was a couple of metres away from her, crouched down, holding a match to a pile of dry kindling that would eventually become a camp-fire. Adrianna tried to sit upright, but slumped back as a wave of dizziness claimed her, a moan escaping her lips.

Bully came over and nuzzled her hand.

Bryce walked over and handed her a flask, his face in darkness with his back towards the flickering flames. 'Here, sip this water . . . I have to get this fire going properly, before we freeze. Will you be all right to lie there a bit longer?'

'Yes,' she said weakly.

But he didn't leave. He just stood there and stared down at her. 'You collapsed,' he said simply.

'I know.'

'It was all too much for you.'

'Probably.'

There was a short sharp silence.

'I'm sorry, Adrianna.'

'I am too,' she managed, a lump in her throat, tears scalding her eyes. Suddenly it was all too much for her and she began to cry, deep racking sobs that tore through her tired, aching body.

'Don't!' groaned Bryce. 'Please don't...'

'It's all right,' she gasped out between sobs. 'You don't have to do anything. Just leave me be... Go back to the fire...'

For a second he hesitated, as though unsure what to do. Then he shrugged unhappily and went back to do as she said.

Oddly enough, she fell back to sleep almost immediately, waking some time later to find the fire roaring, and the smell of food cooking. Bryce was sitting in the dirt, idly stirring the iron pots, the light from the flames touching first one side of his face, then the other. He had changed his clothes, she noticed, into a fresh blue shirt and darker jeans. His hair was damp, as though he had been swimming, yet a quick searching glance revealed no nearby waterhole. Not that she could see very far, the glow from the camp-fire only providing a meagre circle of light in the pitch-black dark of a desert night.

Bryce was obviously unaware of her silent scrutiny, for he continued to stare into the fire, his blank bleak gaze showing his mind was far away in another world.

Where? she wondered. With some woman he had left behind? Some country girl who liked and respected him for what he was, who wouldn't hurt him both physically and emotionally as *she* had done? For Adrianna could not deny that the Bryce who had driven them both so mercilessly all day had been

deeply hurt by her stupid and unfathomable behaviour. OK, so his anger was probably based on in-
jured male pride—or an intense sexual frustration—
but that didn't make her actions any less excusable.
She had been playing with the man's feelings, one
moment wanting him, the next rejecting him, and
shame was a heavy load on her heart. It was hardly
the way to treat a man who had saved her life, not
once, but twice!

Looking over at his grimly hunched figure, she resolved to do everything in her power not to annoy or
upset him for the rest of the trip. She would not only
be civil, but she would be decent and pleasant, show
him that she didn't look down on him at all, that she
appreciated what he had done for her.

Her sense of guilt increased when she realised she
had not once asked him about himself and his life,
that she had indeed prejudged him. Not to mention
patronised him. Adrianna groaned as she recalled the
wide-eyed surprise she had displayed when he showed
himself for the intelligent man he really was. Not only
intelligent, but clever and self-sufficient and strong
and caring and . . .

Adrianna brought herself up sharp. Now stop that!
You're making him sound like a cross between Mother
Teresa and St Francis of Assisi. He's not that much
of a saint! Why, he's done a spot of prejudging
himself, hasn't he? And he couldn't have made a
nastier accusation about you if he'd tried, virtually
calling you a two-timing tramp.

Ah, yes, but . . . that inner voice of conscience inserted softly. There was more than a spot of truth in
that accusation, wasn't there? Alan hasn't exactly been
figuring too largely in your thoughts lately, has he?

'Oh, shut up,' she muttered under her breath, and propped herself up on one elbow, all the more determined to act decently. 'Bryce,' she said, wincing slightly when his head jerked round to set hard eyes upon her, 'I . . . er . . . I'm awake.'

'So I see,' was his dry reply.

Her sigh carried genuine regret. 'Let's not be nasty to each other any more, Bryce. I'm sorry for the things I've said. I'm sorry for everything . . .'

He made an exasperated sound, but a wry smile was tugging at his lips. 'My God, let me jot this momentous occasion down in my diary! Adrianna Winslow, saying she was wrong about something!'

'Oh, I didn't say I was wrong,' she countered with a smile of her own. 'I merely said I was sorry I said what I said. After all, look what it got me. A backside that probably won't be able to sit down for a week, let alone ride Humpty-Dumpty!'

It was surprisingly good to hear Bryce laugh again. He tipped back his head and let the happy sounds roll from his throat. They echoed back in the still of the night, bringing some startled barking from Bully. His eyes pricked up when he heard the echo of his own barking and he raced off into the darkness to see where the other dog was.

'That dog of yours is almost as dumb as your camels,' she chuckled.

'But not nearly as dumb as his master,' Bryce said with obviously cryptic intent. Adrianna wisely decided to make no comment.

'At least I was right. We're not too far from the gorge,' he went on. 'There has to be more than sandhills and creek beds to make an echo.'

'What gorge is that?' she asked.

'Just a gorge. It's got an Aboriginal name, but I can't recall what it is. It's too remote and uninspiring to warrant attention for tourists, so it hasn't acquired an English name. An old Abo showed it to me years ago, because he said it was a reliable waterhole. Even in a drought the water doesn't dry up, because it's fed by an underground spring. This year, with the added run-off from the rain, the lagoon will be brimming.'

'You look as if you've already had a swim. Is there a waterhole near here?'

'Unfortunately no, but I thought we weren't far from the gorge, so I used up some of our water supply having a good wash.'

'I wish I had a change of clothes,' Adrianna said with an unhappy glance down at herself. Her linen pants and silk blouse were grimy and dusty, with caught threads and dirty smudges all over them.

'You can wash and dry them at the gorge tomorrow. We'll camp there for the day, if you like; give you a chance to recover.'

'Yes . . . yes, I think we'll have to,' she said thoughtfully. No use pretending she was in a physical state to keep going. As it was, she would have to walk the rest of the way to the gorge. Riding was out of the question.

'Ready for some dinner yet?' he asked.

'Definitely.'

'You'll be pleased to know there's a change of menu. Pasta and tinned sauce, followed by fruit salad splashed with some of that brandy and long-life cream.'

'Mmm,' she sighed. 'Sounds marvellous!'

Bryce brought a steaming plateful of the Italian-smelling dish over and she pulled herself upright to sit on the relative softness of the lumpy pillow, having

to bite her tongue to stop a groan from escaping. She
must have looked pained, however.

'I'll give you some horse liniment later,' he offered
as he handed over the plate. 'Rub it in wherever it
hurts.'

'In that case I hope you've got a bucketful!'

His downward glance held reluctant amusement.
'You know, Adrianna, you can be really nice when
you want to be.'

'Goodness, let me jot this momentous occasion
down in my diary,' she retorted, in a parody of what
he'd said earlier. 'Bryce McLean, saying something
nice about me!'

He laughed. 'You're too smart for your own good,
do you know that?'

'Yes,' she said with a rueful dryness. It was exactly
what her father had said when she'd gained a really
good pass in the Higher School Certificate, despite
having missed countless days.

'I can't stand smart women,' Bryce added, still
smiling.

'I don't wonder,' she returned.

His eyes flashed and there was a split second when
the situation might have got sticky. But Bryce quickly
relaxed into a grin. 'I've been wondering,' he drawled,
'just what you do for a living. Now I think I know.
You're one of those lady lawyers who go into a
courtroom, oozing sweet smiles and ultra-feminine
glamour, just to instil the opposite side with a false
sense of confidence, then, when the defendant is in
the box, whammo! That acid tongue and steel-trap
mind of yours goes to work and the poor bastard gets
so mixed up he ends up dobbing himself in.'

Adrianna giggled and shook her head.

'No? Let's see...what else is there? Public relations? Super-secretary?'

Again she smiled and shook her head.

'If you tell me you're a check-out chick I won't believe it!'

Now she laughed outright. 'Actually, I was a check-out chick for three years while I was going through college.'

'If so then I bet all the other girls in the supermarket hated you. I'll bet you scanned all those items so fast you made them look like they were standing still.'

He was right, actually. In the end, she had learnt not to be so efficient, rather than endure the vicious looks and jealous comments from the other women.

'Well?' he prompted. 'Are you going to tell me what you did at college?'

'I will, *after* I've eaten this delicious food.'

'I'll keep you to that,' he warned, and walked off to hobble the camels for the night.

Adrianna watched him work while she ate, recalling how she had first thought that hobbling meant tying up—to a tree or something similar. But it wasn't like that at all. Both the camels wore leather cuffs low down on their front legs which Bryce linked together every night with chains. Each chain was only a foot long, which allowed them the freedom to walk and graze but not to wander or run off too far.

After hobbling the camels, Bryce fed Bully, then rejoined her with the promised dessert, settling down on a blanket next to her and doggedly returning to his earlier questioning about what she did for a living.

'I have a fashion business,' she told him. 'I design a range of women's wear under my own personal label, and I own a few boutiques that stock them exclusively.'

He looked surprised. 'I'd never have guessed it. I would have thought you'd do something more intellectual.'

'There's very little money in being intellectual.'

One of Bryce's eyebrows lifted. 'That sounded cynical.'

'I guess I am a bit,' she murmured, and spooned some of the delicious fruit salad and cream into her mouth.

'How does one go about becoming a fashion designer and boutique owner?' Bryce asked after he'd reduced his dessert considerably with a couple of huge mouthfuls.

With some pauses for eating, Adrianna patiently revealed that after leaving school she had taken a textiles and design course at a Sydney college, after which she had secured a job as assistant to the designer in a minor fashion house. Even then she had continued her studies at night, doing a managerial and business administration course. By the time this second diploma was completed, she was twenty-three, and ready to go out on her own.

'I knew I'd never get rich working for wages,' she commented, 'something I learnt from the lady my mother used to do cleaning for. I think I was around fifteen when Mum came home one day and repeated what her employer had said.'

You'll never get anywhere, Flo, working for so much an hour for someone else. You should start a company that supplies cleaners, send other women out on cleaning jobs and collect a commission!

'Mum laughed,' Adrianna explained, 'but I thought the idea brilliant. It came to me then that I would have my own business one day. So once I was properly qualified, and had saved up enough money to back myself, I did just that!'

'And made a success of it, I'll warrant,' came Bryce's comment.

'Well, yes, I have...'

He gave her a long, penetrating look. 'Tell me,' he said at last, 'is it so important for you to be rich?'

She gave the question honest consideration. 'I don't want to be too rich,' was her thoughtful and frowning answer. 'Being too rich means a loss of privacy. But I want to have enough money to be my own person, to not have to depend on any man for my next meal.'

'Then why are you marrying Alan Carstairs?' Bryce asked, frowning.

Adrianna took a deep breath, and battened down the hatches on her sudden rise in blood-pressure. Of course a man like Bryce would equate marriage with a woman giving up her independence. Most men did. Still, she didn't want another slanging match with him, and she resolved to answer carefully.

'Alan and I are friends, Bryce. We like and respect each other. And we both want the same things in life.'

'Which are?'

'A satisfying career and a life partner to share things with but who will still give their respective spouses the right to do and be what they want to be.'

'You didn't say anything about having a family.'

Adrianna stiffened. 'No,' she said tautly, 'I didn't.'

'You don't want children?'

'No.'

'I can understand why Carstairs wouldn't want them—he wouldn't want to be put to the trouble. But why don't you want them, Adrianna?'

She set reproachful eyes on him. 'Will you please stop sneering about Alan? After all, weren't you the person who accused me of prejudice? You don't really know Alan, you know. Not the man he is now. So you can't say what his reasons are for not wanting children. As for my reasons, I just don't think I'd make a very good mother.'

'Why not?'

'Oh, for heaven's sake!'

'That's what I say. Fancy deciding not to have children for such a silly reason! A lot of women think they won't make good mothers, but after they've actually had a baby, all those suppressed maternal feelings suddenly burst into life.'

'I doubt it,' was her dry comment.

'Why do you say that?'

Adrianna rolled her eyes. 'Will you kindly drop this subject?'

'No.'

She glared at his determined face. 'Because I've been there before and I didn't like it,' she snapped.

He was clearly taken aback. 'You've *had* a baby?'

'No,' she sighed impatiently. 'Oh, good grief, I suppose I'll just have to tell you everything to shut you up.'

He sat perfectly still, looking at her intently as she began telling him as quickly and impersonally as possible all about her growing-up years, about her frustrations and resentments, her near-miss violence with her baby brothers, her contempt for her father, her pity for her mother. Of course she couldn't keep up the cold matter-of-fact tone. After a while her voice started vibrating with emotion and once or twice words caught in her throat.

Yet somehow in the soothing quiet of the desert night, the words kept spilling out, on and on. It was like a catharsis of all those bitter years, a cleansing of her soul.

'I left home immediately after I did my HSC,' she concluded. 'Dad followed me and demanded that I come back and help support the family. I looked him straight in the eye and told him what I thought of him, that I had no intention of letting him take any of the money *I* earnt for grog and gambling; I told him he was a useless, hopeless rotten excuse for a husband and father and I never wanted to see him again.'

'Wow!' Bryce exclaimed, but his eyes showed respect. 'That temper of yours isn't new, then.'

She gave him a shaky look, her whole being trembling inside with spent emotion. 'No, I guess not . . .' Yet oddly enough, in the last few years she had kept it well under control. It had only been here, in the desert with Bryce, that it seemed to have reared its ugly head again.

'You did the right thing,' he said with gentle understanding.

She didn't make any comment to that, her chin quivering dangerously as tears pricked her eyes. *Had* she done the right thing? Would she ever get over the guilt of leaving her mother behind? Yet she had begged her mother to come with her, but she wouldn't. Her spirit had been long crushed. Adrianna's only comfort had been that her mother had been set free eventually, by her father's death. Even then her mother had refused to come and live with her, deciding to spend the rest of her life looking after sons who were proving as useless and parasitic as their father.

'Come along, don't cry now and spoil your image,' Bryce warned.

She had to laugh. 'No need to ask what image that is, I suppose.'

'Ask away, I'll tell you.'

She sighed. 'All right, tell me. I can take it.'

He smiled at her. 'That's just it.'

'What?' she asked, confused.

'The fact that you can take it. I'd say you can take an awful lot without cracking. You're a strong and very courageous woman, Adrianna Winslow. A rare woman...'

Adrianna stared at his openly admiring face, then quickly dropped her lashes. 'Don't, Bryce,' she choked out.

'Don't what?'

'Don't like me. And don't make me like you back. I...I can't handle it. I...' Her hand shook violently as she lowered the now empty plate to the blanket. She closed her eyes tightly. 'I love Alan and I'm going to marry him,' she lied.

When she opened her eyes again, it was to find Bryce frowning at her. Gradually the frown cleared and he nodded slowly. 'It's all right, Adrianna,' he said soothingly. 'It's all right. Don't upset yourself so.'

'But it's not all right!' she cried, lifting her hands up to hide her weeping from him. 'I *do* like you. I *do*...'

A silence fell between them—an electric silence. The seconds ticked away as agonisingly as they would during an atom-bomb countdown, with Adrianna petrified that her admission would make Bryce do something foolish, something they would both regret later. If he touched her or kissed her...

Her eyes flew open in a panic when she heard Bryce get to his feet. She stared up at him, her face filled with both fear and an awful excited churning. What was he going to do?

But he merely shook his head. Picking up the blanket, he walked slowly around to the other side of the camp and dropped it to the ground. 'Goodnight, Adrianna,' he called across the fire, his voice sounding terribly tired. 'Sleep well.'

'Good...goodnight,' she answered weakly.

And oddly enough, she did sleep well, emotional and physical exhaustion eventually taking their toll. But before her mind was snatched into oblivion it whirled and whirled, tortured by thoughts that she would rather not have had.

I wouldn't have stopped him, she kept thinking, if he'd wanted me.

But the worst realisation was that he hadn't wanted her. Not any more.

CHAPTER SEVEN

THERE were no disturbing thoughts or feelings, however, when Adrianna woke the next morning. It was hard to concentrate on anything other than pain when one's muscles had set during the night into hard, twisted knots of agony.

She struggled out of the bedroll and tried to straighten, with little success. Hands on hips and teeth gritted, she finally managed it, flexing her shoulder-blades back and forth till she had some of the crinks out. But of course it was her lower half that presented the worst of her troubles. Her thighs and bottom, to be precise.

A brisk hand-rub on the latter and a couple of knee bends loosened her up a fraction, then she took a quiet stroll around, careful not to wake Bryce, who was still sound asleep. Bully joined her, his beady black eyes looking up at her every now and then whenever she groaned.

'I'd pat you,' she told the dog, 'if I didn't think you'd bite my hand off.'

Bully gave a low growl as though he agreed with her. They walked along ahead for a while, with Adrianna looking for a sight of the gorge. But the creek-bed twisted and turned, the lining of large leafy eucalyptus trees obscuring any long-distance view, so eventually she turned around and went back to the camp, finding Bryce up and busy with breakfast. He hadn't shaved yet, but the stubbly chin didn't look bad on him. In fact, he looked too damned attractive all over, his chest-hugging shirt and body-moulding jeans leaving little of his impressive male frame to the imagination.

Adrianna tensed up as she drew near, and when Bryce looked over his shoulder and sent her one of his lazy grins, her whole insides did a somersault.

'Feeling better this morning?' he asked, and stood up straight, stretching wide with a yawn.

'Yes,' was her one-word, almost curt reply.

'Still stiff, by the way you were walking. I forgot to give you that liniment—sorry.'

He gave her such a warm, caring look that Adrianna tensed even further. She shouldn't have admitted to liking him or told him so much about herself. Those kinds of revelations broke down barriers between people, barriers she would have preferred to be still firmly in place.

'It doesn't matter,' she said sharply. 'I'll loosen up in the walk to the gorge. Riding is out of the question, I'm afraid.'

'That bad, eh?' he said, apparently thinking her snappy tone was the result of discomfort. 'Oh, well, it's not far.' He bent then and lifted the lid on the large iron pot in the middle of the smouldering fire, and a delicious smell wafted up to hit Adrianna's nostrils. Quite involuntarily she drew in a deep breath and sighed sensuously.

'Fantastic smell, isn't it?' he drawled. 'There's nothing better than damper for breakfast on a crisp desert morning.'

Adrianna's mouth was practically watering as Bryce scooped the circular, bread-like loaf out of the pot on to a large plate.

'It's certainly of bribable quality,' she commented.

His sideways glance had an amused twinkle in it. '*How* bribable?'

'Not *that* bribable!' she shot back.

He laughed. 'You don't know what I was suggesting?'

'It doesn't take a genius to guess.'

He pretended to look offended. 'Oh, Adrianna, I'm wounded.'

'You will be if you try anything,' she snapped.

He held the lid of the iron pot in front of his groin. 'Go ahead,' he teased. 'See if I care!'

A reluctant giggle came to her throat.

'My God, Bully, did you hear that?' Bryce cried in mock horror.

The dog cocked his head on one side, looking so silly that Adrianna burst out laughing.

'Good grief, now she's getting hysterical. It must be hunger. Here, I'd better give her some of this damper, Bully, before she goes over the edge.'

Despite her repeated laughter, Adrianna found breakfast oddly unnerving. When in good humour Bryce was a charming and amusing companion. That and his macho sex appeal were a lethal combination and she found it hard to stop herself looking at him with both affection and desire. However, when on one occasion she caught him staring at her quite speculatively, she quickly fashioned her face into a cool expression and asked whether, if they made their stop at the gorge a brief one, it was possible to reach Dover Downs before nightfall.

Bryce gave her a frowning look. 'In case you haven't noticed, the camels are done in,' he said, his tone puzzled and almost angry. 'They need a rest. I thought you did too.'

Her agitated sigh drew a darker frown from him this time, but he said nothing. 'It was just an idea,' she muttered.

'Is my company so obnoxious to you?' he asked, clearly irritated.

'You know it isn't,' she said unhappily.

'I won't make a pass at you, you know.'

She stiffened. 'I realise that.'

'Is that what's bothering you? That I *won't*?'

Her mouth dropped open, her cheeks flushing guiltily.

He swore and spun away from her. 'Be ready to leave in half an hour,' he snapped over his shoulder. 'We'll reach Dover Downs today if it kills the bloody lot of us!'

It took them less than half an hour of quick walking across the open plain to reach the gorge. Half an hour of incredible heat burning up through the soles of Adrianna's sandals. Half an hour of complaining muscles and gritted teeth and uncomfortable silence.

But she forgot her wretchedness for a moment when the gorge came into view.

It was, quite literally, stunningly beautiful. Not picture-pretty, as the oasis had been, but far more impressive. A large expanse of blue-green water, edged with enormous yellow ochre rocks on two sides, a small sandy beach down the shallow end, and the gorge at the other. Down there, the waters looked very deep, becoming black and crystalline as they flowed through a ravine less than ten feet wide and seemingly endless, red and black cliffs rising sheer out of the water on either side.

'Why, it's magnificent!' she exclaimed.

'It is, isn't it?' Bryce agreed softly.

She swallowed as she looked over at him, his gentle tone catching at her heart-strings. This was another side of him she hadn't really appreciated till now, this softer, gentler side, this lover of animals and nature. It unravelled all her defences, making her feel mixed up inside as she yearned to reach out to him. 'Bryce, I...'

Her words broke off when she saw his eyes harden. 'No,' he snarled. 'No apologies, no making up, no nothing any more! I've had enough, Adrianna. I'm not a puppet who can be pulled this way and that depending how you feel at the moment. I'm a man, and by God, if you don't watch it, I'll give you a memorable demonstration of that fact! And believe me, it won't be rape. We both know that, don't we?'

She watched with chest contracting and heart aflutter as he grabbed both camels' reins and stalked off in the direction of a large acacia tree. Before she could think what to do, he dragged the checked blanket off Dumbo's saddle, let the camels go and stalked back towards her. She just stood there, frozen by the aura of simmering violence in his angry approach. He stopped a couple of yards from her, eyes ablaze.

'We'll start out for Dover Downs after lunch,' he ground out. 'That gives you three hours to rest and wash and dry your clothes. 'Here...' he threw the blanket at her feet '...take this with you so that you can use it as cover till your clothes dry. May I suggest for the sake of all concerned that you keep to one side of the lagoon while I keep to the other, since we'll both be swimming in the raw.'

'I...I'll need some soap,' she said shakily.

'It's in one of the bottom packs,' he growled. 'And for pity's sake don't offer to help me find it. I'll get it for you after I've attended to the camels and cooled off a bit. I suggest you do the same. You look almost as hot as I feel!' He whirled on his heels then and marched off.

She glared after him for a second, furious with him. And herself. She didn't deserve to be treated this way! And yet she supposed that after all that had happened, any attempt of hers to be nice *might* have looked like some pathetic ploy to seduce him. Muttering her exasperation, she snatched the blanket up and strode off in the direction of the far side of the gorge, thinking that Dover Downs could not come quickly enough.

Though to be honest, she wasn't looking forward to seeing Alan again, to telling him that not only did she not want to marry him, but that she didn't want to continue their affair either. Alan deserved better than a half-hearted wife—or lover—which was what she would be after this experience. It would be a long time before she would get Bryce out of her mind, her heart, and her body.

She finally came to a spot where the rocks were large and smooth, dipping gently down to the water's edge. It was the ideal natural ramp from which to slide into the water, letting the blanket go at the last moment, then scooping it up on exiting.

An agitated glance back in the direction of the camp showed that Bryce's back was to her, so she quickly divested herself of all her clothes and slipped into the water. The unexpected coldness took her breath away and it was several minutes before she got used to it, several minutes of consciously not looking either back at the camp or across at the other side, in case by this time Bryce was there, undressing. Adrianna didn't think that a long-distance view of a man's naked body would disturb her too much, but she wasn't taking any chances. Besides, if Bryce caught her looking at him he would probably accuse her of ogling him on purpose.

Even so, when she actually heard the splash of someone diving into the water a sliver of shocking awareness rippled through her. It was hard not to picture Bryce's nude body slicing through the water, very hard *not* to want to look over at him, even if he was at least a hundred yards away.

She didn't deliberately look his way. But the sound of Bully's barking drew her attention and out of the corner of her eye she was surprised to see Bryce already leaving the water, the dog dancing around his master's dripping legs. She was instantly dry-mouthed as she watched Bryce bend over and pick up his jeans. His actions looked angry as he inserted each leg, then pulled them on over his glistening buttocks. Not glancing back, he scooped up the rest of his clothes and began to stride, bare-chested, back towards the camp.

Dragging her eyes away, Adrianna trod water for a while, trying to control the body responses she was beginning to hate—the quickened heartbeat, the flush of heat, the surge of erotic visions. With her unfortunate feelings and thoughts finally dampened down she had just decided to get out herself when a cramp struck her foot.

Not panicking, she quickly side-stroked over to the rock, only to find it was far easier to get in than to get out, the rock surface under the waterline scooping inwards and being covered in slippery moss. She struggled to find a foothold, but there weren't any. Then she tried spreading her arms wide and digging her elbows downwards in an attempt to lever herself up on to the rock, but in her weakened state she didn't have the strength to overcome the dragging weight of the water.

She was in considerable pain and beginning to feel definite alarm when Bryce's bare feet appeared on the blanket in front of her. An upward glance saw him standing, still disconcertingly bare-chested, looking down at her with black humour in his eyes.

'Having trouble?' he drawled.

'Yes, I . . . I can't seem to get a foothold.'

'It's quite easy to get out on the other side,' he mocked. 'Swim over there. I'll take this soap and your blanket over for you.' He went to pick up the blanket, but didn't, straightening to give her a knowingly malicious smile. 'Or were you expecting me to help you out?'

'Well, no, but I . . . I don't think I can make it over there,' she gasped. 'I have cramp.'

His laugh was cold and cruel. 'In that case you'll just have to drown, won't you?'

She grimaced as the cramp worsened, looking over at the other side with a sinking heart. It was too far. . .

His expression remained ruthless. 'If you think I'm going to haul you out of that water as naked as a jaybird and then just walk away, you're a fool, Adrianna Winslow! You've been putting me through hell, and I'm not in the mood to be merciful any longer!'

She stared up at where his arousal was clearly outlined against the damp denim of his jeans. Her eyes shot up to his face, only to find his own gaze roving hotly over her bare shoulders. Then lower. . .

To have him look at her naked breasts that way, even through the distortion of the rippling water, was incredibly exciting.

'It's up to you, Adrianna,' he ground out, and bent forward, throwing the cake of soap behind him and sending a tempting hand downwards. 'You can either take your chances with the water. Or with me. But be warned, I'd choose the water if I were you!'

CHAPTER EIGHT

HER hand shook as she placed it in the large palm, but her eyes were oddly steady, meeting his with a flash of fire. She had decided, even if she had to suffer for it for the rest of her life.

'So!' he said, his surprise quickly replaced by a triumphant smile. His hand slipped past her trembling fingers to close around her wrist and he lifted her as if she was a feather, lifted and deposited her next to him in one fluid movement.

His eyes swept over her dripping nudity with an all-encompassing regard, returning to her face with a look of such passion that it took her breath away. 'I knew you were beautiful,' he rasped, 'but I didn't know how much.'

Adrianna stared back at him, thinking dazedly that she could not say the same in return. To describe him as beautiful would be totally inadequate. He was magnificent, breathtaking. The supreme male animal... As perfectly shaped as a David or an Adonis, but larger, stronger, harder! What had he said to her once? When he took her, she would know she'd been taken by a man! Her throat went dry just thinking about it.

Another spasm in her right foot brought a whimper of pain.

'Do you honestly think that ploy will work?' Bryce snarled. 'I won't have pity on you, you know. It's gone too far for pity!'

She winced again with the pain and lifted her foot slightly, pressing her toes hard against the rock, trying to unravel the cramp. A slow, wicked smile sliced across his broodingly handsome face and he dropped to one knee, picking the foot up and massaging it with exquisite skill. Adrianna almost overbalanced, putting her hands on to his shoulders so that she didn't tip back into the water.

'You have the sexiest little feet,' he murmured, his thumbs kneading the pain away and sending a thousand electric shivers charging along her nerve-endings.

Adrianna gazed down at him through a type of erotic haze. Quite unbidden, her hands began to slide back and forth across his broad strong shoulders in a journey of sensual satisfaction. A low moan whispered from her lips.

His upward glance was heavy-lidded as he continued to massage the sole of her foot. 'You like that, don't you?' he said thickly.

She blinked down at him, eyes wide, lips falling slightly apart. Never in all her life had she envisaged the sort of feelings this man could make her feel. Anything—even the slightest touch—excited her unbearably, sending her insides twisting into a tight ball of excruciating need.

'Yes,' she breathed. 'Yes . . .'

'And this?' He placed her foot back down and slid his hands up her legs, caressing the backs of her knees, then sliding upwards to linger on the soft flesh of her thighs.

Adrianna sucked in a deep breath and held it. 'Yes,' she choked out.

'And this . . .' His feathering fingers found more intimate targets. She gasped aloud, and began to sink downwards.

Somehow they both ended up kneeling, facing each other on the blanket, Adrianna's chin tipped up so that she could keep looking into his smouldering eyes. It was like a drug to have them staring into hers, holding her while his hands explored and aroused her to fever pitch.

'Tell me what else you like,' he whispered, his hands abandoning their devastating caresses to slide up over her stomach towards her breasts.

'Anything,' she said, her voice shaking as she struggled for breath, her cheeks raging with the heat of excitement and desire.

His hands lifted off her quivering expectant body to cup her face, his mouth smiling as it began to bend. 'That's a very open invitation, Adrianna . . . Are you sure you mean *anything*?'

It was clearly a rhetorical question, for he cut off any answer with a kiss, an open-mouthed yet oddly gentle kiss that still sent her head spinning. She made a tiny sound of disappointment when the soft sucking of her lips ended.

'More?' he murmured seductively.

She nodded numbly, aware that her heart was beating so fast she thought it would burst.

With his thumbs massaging the corners of her mouth he began by moistening her lips with his tongue, running the tip over them till they were soft and pouting and tingling. The thumbs retreated to her cheeks then, allowing his mouth an unimpeded possession. His lips pressed on to hers, then parted, taking hers with him. Once they were open for him, he sent his tongue forward to play sensuously and slowly with hers, then darted back to his own warm moist cavern so that she ached with the desertion and sent her own tongue forward.

It was a game, a sexy game of foray and retreat that took all Adrianna's attention and left her unknowing that the rest of her body was responding as wildly and fiercely as her mouth. Her breasts were swelling to an engorged sensitivity, her nipples rocklike in readiness for further erotic play. Unbeknown to her fevered brain, the hard points were already brushing against Bryce's chest, sending electric impulses to other parts of her body, other parts which were flooding with a liquid heat.

At long last Bryce stopped kissing her and laid her trembling body back on the blanket, parting her thighs and bending his mouth to where she was already a cauldron of fire. She cried out in some sort of vague protest, groaning as she felt her body rushing towards a climax. Quite abruptly he abandoned her, getting up to stand at her feet, holding her madly dilated eyes with his while he stripped off his jeans. Her eyes grew even wider as she saw him in all his naked glory, wondering if her slender body could encompass such a man.

'Don't look so worried,' he soothed as he stretched out beside her. 'We'll be perfect together. Now...where was I? Ah yes, I remember. Let's try something less stressful, shall we?' And he bent his head and starting licking one of her nipples.

Adrianna had to bite her bottom lip to stop the moans. But when he kept doing it and at the same time slid a hand down between her thighs, she could not contain a convulsive shudder.

'God, you're so hot in there...so hot...'

Adrianna shut her eyes tight, her insides squeezing just as tight against the sensations that were rocketing through her. 'Oh, Bryce!' she cried, her hips lifting to writhe against his devastatingly intimate caress.

'Yes?'

'Please...' Her breath was coming in rapid panting gasps. 'Don't keep doing that. Please... I can't bear it... make love to me... properly... now... I don't want to... to...'

He stopped immediately, taking her hands and surprising her by pulling her to her feet. 'That rock's too hard on your back,' he said thickly. 'Here... When I lift you put your arms tightly around my neck.'

His hands slid down to span her buttocks, lifting her with ease, her thighs falling either side of his hips quite naturally. Her arms went up around his neck, her elbows resting on his shoulders, her fingers splaying up into his damp, spiked hair. For a second he clasped her to him, burying his face into the valley between her breasts, but then he was holding her away, positioning her so that his manhood probed at her soft, moist flesh. Then in a slow sensuous sheathing he pulled her down on to him, the sensation of his filling her to capacity taking her breath away.

It seemed to take his breath away too, for he sank to his knees, gasping and closing his eyes for a few seconds. She wrapped her legs tightly around him and pressed her lips to his right ear. 'Oh, my darling,' she murmured softly. 'My darling...'

He groaned at her endearment and she slid her lips across to cover his mouth. He sank back on his heels and while she was kissing him he began to move her, slowly, easing her away, then pulling her back down on to him till she engulfed every inch of his throbbing manhood once more. It was the most erotic, the most tormenting mating, as he refused to be hurried, even by her groans of impatience. He even stopped once, lifting his mouth from hers and looking deep into her glazed eyes, his own heavy with passion.

'Now you're mine, Adrianna,' he rasped. 'Mine...'

'Yes, my darling, yes,' she agreed, her head tipping back, lips parted with excitement.

He made some sort of sound, then taking the back of her head in a savage grip, he pulled her hungrily back to his mouth, thrusting his tongue inside with a sudden ferocity. Just as abruptly he abandoned the kiss to clasp her hips again, his fingers digging into her soft flesh as the rhythm of his hands rapidly reached a frenzied pitch. Adrianna's low moans became whimpering cries, then gasping groans, her whole being besieged by a wild combination of sensation and tension. The feelings of pleasure and pressure spiralled upwards, totally out of control. It wasn't just him moving her now. She had joined his urgency in a frantic feverish ride.

'Oh, Bryce...Bryce!' she gasped, sensing her body on the knife-edge of ecstasy. And then it was happening, her climax exceeding even her wildest expectations, her fierce contractions convulsing around him and sending his seed spilling into her with a strength that tore a loud cry from deep within his throat. She clasped his shuddering body close, hers still moving, savouring every last erotic nuance of feeling she could experience.

But finally, reluctantly, the heat of passion ebbed from her body, replaced by a swimming sensation of utter satisfaction and contentment. She sighed and slumped downwards, her arms around his chest, her head tucked under his neck. His lips moved lovingly over her hair and she felt his breath like a warm breeze down the back of her neck. They stayed that way for some time, rocking slightly, holding each other, enjoying the moment of total intimacy and tender joy.

Adrianna felt the beginnings of apprehension the second Bryce lifted his head. She just *knew* he was going to say something to spoil the illusion of happiness she had been basking in.

'You can't marry Carstairs now,' he said, almost accusingly.

Adrianna groaned inside. That was it ... This was where it would all begin... The demands...the telling her what she could and could not do, all because she had betrayed her love for him with her body.

She sucked in a startled breath, her head snapping up to stare at him. My God, what did I just say to myself? she thought. I can't love him, not really. It has to be just sex. It has to be.

But of course she knew it wasn't.

'No,' she admitted on a shaky sigh, 'I'm not going to marry Alan now.'

She saw the look of triumphant relief flash across Bryce's blue eyes and wondered if he loved her back. But only for a second. Physical men like Bryce didn't *really* love. When they said they loved it usually meant they desired or wanted or needed. They married girls when they thought they loved them, only to have unlimited access to their bodies, but they quickly grew bored and began looking elsewhere for their pleasure. The trouble was, by then a baby had usually made an appearance.

'I won't marry you either, Bryce,' she added before he could say another word. 'We're not right for each other.'

His face darkened. 'You can say that while we are as we are?' he grated, giving her a savage yank to remind her of their extremely intimate position. 'We *love* each other.'

'Don't, Bryce,' she said in a strangled voice.

'Don't what, Adrianna?' His voice was low and taunting. 'Don't mention the word love? Or don't make love to you? Perhaps I should remind you of what you said in the heat of your passion . . . You said you would be mine, my love. Would you like to tell me in what way you meant that?'

Adrianna refused to say a word.

'You meant just sexually, didn't you?' he snarled. 'That's all you want from me, isn't it? Not my love or anything else I might be able to give you. And the ironic thing is I *can* give you more,' he added in a type of pained desperation. 'Much more than your narrow-minded view of me decided at first sight.' His eyes blazed as they raked over her flushed face. 'God damn you, Adrianna! God damn you!'

She was taken aback and distressed by the depth of his emotion and fury. Perhaps he did really love her, and perhaps he imagined he could somehow make a decent life for her out here in the outback. But if he thought *she* had spoken in the heat of passion, then wasn't he doing the same? What of their future in the cold light of day, when it became obvious that they had nothing in common, that she would not buckle under and become a domestic slave, that the only thing they *did* have together was good sex.

Yet despite her common-sense reasoning, she ached to put her arms around him again, to soothe his anger, to tell him she did love him and she would be his forever. Adrianna shook her head, amazed. A few days ago she would never have dreamt of doing such a thing. Maybe Bryce was right when he'd said the desert changed people. It had certainly changed her,

so much so that she was almost hoping she had con-
ceived a child a few minutes ago. Maybe she couldn't
come to terms with living in the outback, but somehow
the idea of a baby—Bryce's baby—wasn't so
abhorrent to her. It was, in fact, very attractive. Which
was amazing really...

'And what does that shake of the head mean?'
Bryce said coldly.

'Oh, Bryce...Bryce,' she cried softly, slipping her
arms around his waist. 'I feel so mixed up.' She lifted
unhappy eyes to him and couldn't bear to see the dis-
illusionment and derision in his face. 'I *do* love
you...I *do*!' And she hugged him and pressed her
lips to his chest, raining kisses over his skin.

She felt him shudder, but when she looked up she
wasn't ready for the look in his eyes. It was
so...*happy*! He kept gazing down at her, but then a
slight wariness slipped into his eyes and he too shook
his head. 'You don't know what you want, do you?'
he said indulgently.

'I know I want *you*,' she husked. 'But, Bryce, please
try to understand. Marriage between us...it...it
probably wouldn't work out.'

He stared down at her for a long time and she
became faintly worried by the unreadable expression
that clouded his normally expressive and open eyes.
It was as though he were deliberately hiding his
feelings from her. 'I think you're right,' he pronounced carefully at last. 'A marriage between us is
doomed to fail.'

'It...it *is*?' she repeated, feeling perversely hurt that
he agreed with her, that he wasn't even going to try
to persuade her.

'It couldn't work at all,' he went on. 'For one thing you don't want children. Any woman I marry would at least want to have one child.'

'Oh . . . well, Bryce, I . . .'

'Not only that, you're a city girl,' he cut in firmly. 'You wouldn't be able to stand life out here. The heat, the dust, the flies, the loneliness, would all get to you after a while. And as for me . . . I couldn't stand the hustle and bustle of the city. Not permanently. It would be a funny marriage with us living hundreds of miles apart and no children.'

'Yes . . . I guess so, but . . .'

'There's no use talking about buts, Adrianna,' he said. 'Facts are facts. The more I think about it, I don't want to marry you, any more than you want to marry me. It's only common sense—I can see that now. Still, there does seem to be one thing we do want from each other, doesn't there?'

And he silenced any further arguments with a kiss, which was just as well, Adrianna thought dazedly, for she'd been about to say that she had changed her mind about all those things; that she would give up her career, she would live wherever he lived, she would have a dozen children by him!

Good lord, what was getting into her? Was she going the same way as her mother, letting the seductive power of physical pleasure colour her thinking? Yet it was so hard to think straight when Bryce was kissing her, when already she could feel his body stirring to arousal again.

Oh God . . . It wasn't just Bryce who was getting turned on again, Adrianna soon realised. Already the desire to move, to feel his growing hardness, was becoming impossible to ignore. With a sensuous sigh she surrendered to it, lifting her body and sinking

back, revelling in the glorious feeling of his rapidly
swelling desire. Again she did it. And again.

Bryce groaned, his mouth leaving hers to trail
moistly down her throat, then slide back up to blow
gently in her ear, making her shiver uncontrollably.

'Let's not talk about the future just now,' he
husked. 'Here...at this moment...there's no outside
world, no tomorrow. Just you and me, like this. We
have something very special together, Adrianna. Let's
enjoy that, at least for now. Forget everything else
but touching and kissing and making love, over and
over and over...'

'Oh, yes, Bryce,' she said with a shudder of wild,
wanton delight. 'Yes!'

It was a wonderful, exciting, bewildering day for
Adrianna.

Bryce refused to do anything except make love, with
the occasional break for refreshments. All thinking
and talking was banned, he commanded, except for
love talk and banal comments like, 'Isn't the water
cold?' and 'What shall we have to drink?'

Adrianna found herself taken to a level of sensuality she hadn't thought existed, each lovemaking
session seemingly satisfying her, but leaving her still
half aroused and even more heart-stoppingly aware
of Bryce. She could not seem to keep her hands off
him—nor he off her, for that matter—and they spent
countless hours, touching and caressing each other,
in the water and out, their hands and mouths seemingly never still as they sought out the many various
ways of pleasuring each other.

It was both a revelation and a vague concern to
Adrianna that she would find nothing off-putting in
forms of erotic play she would have previously shrunk

from. If truth be told, she was often more turned on by what she did to Bryce than the other way around. He certainly enjoyed her ministrations too, finding obvious satisfaction when she confessed on one such occasion to never having done such things before.

'Then you're truly mine,' he murmured at this confession, reaching down and running his fingers through her hair till she lifted her face up to look adoringly at him.

The sight of his heavy-lidded, desire-filled eyes brought a sense of pleasure and power that she found incredibly exciting. She continued her highly intimate love-play for several seconds, then glanced up at him again. 'Do you like it when I do that?' she murmured.

He touched her swollen and highly sensitised lips with a loving, possessive touch. 'I love everything you do to me...'

She returned her attentions to his aroused flesh, revelling in his groans of ecstasy, quite deliberately and lovingly choosing to continue till he was totally out of control and there was no turning back.

'You're thinking,' Bryce murmured in an accusing tone.

Adrianna glanced up at him from where she was lying in the crook of his arm, a faint frown marring her otherwise smooth and contented face. 'I can't help it. Today has been incredible, Bryce. But tomorrow will come... And I don't want it to.' She gave a little shiver and put her head back on his arm to stare up at the stars twinkling in the black night sky.

'You're not worried about getting pregnant, are you, Adrianna?' he asked softly.

Her heart skipped a beat. In all honesty she had not given a thought to pregnancy all day. It just showed how an intelligent woman could quite easily fall pregnant when in love. But Bryce's question reminded her that he couldn't have known it was a relatively safe time of the month for her, and she felt slightly uneasy that he hadn't mentioned it earlier. Surely he hadn't been trying to get her pregnant, had he, to force her to marry him? She couldn't get out of her mind the moment when he had closed his thoughts to her, as if he had some secret plan of action he didn't want her to know.

'No,' she said, frowning.

'Sure?' he persisted.

'Positive.'

'How?'

'Trust me,' she almost snapped.

His sigh was telling.

'I . . . I'm sorry, Bryce. It's just that . . .'

'It's all right,' he soothed. 'To be honest, I didn't think about it earlier and I should have. It was stupid and thoughtless of me, and I'm sorry. When is your period due?'

Adrianna flinched away from such personal talk—which was silly after what they had both been doing that day. What could have been more personal than that?

'In a few days,' she admitted stiffly.

'Just as well we're getting you back to civilisation, then, isn't it?'

'Yes . . . yes, I suppose so.'

'You don't sound so sure?'

'I guess I'm not looking forward to seeing Alan again.'

She felt Bryce tense. 'What are you going to tell him?'

Adrianna swallowed. 'The truth.'

'Which is?'

'That I can't marry him, that I've fallen in love with someone else.'

'*And*?' Bryce grated.

'And what?' she asked, twisting round to look up at him again.

'And you won't be seeing him again. Ever!'

Adrianna sat upright, her anger swift and strong. 'Oh, yes, I will, Bryce McLean. Alan was my friend long before he became my lover. I won't throw him away just because I happen to have fallen in love with you!'

Bryce glared back at her, his eyes narrow, his jaw clenched hard. Then suddenly he seemed to make a conscious effort to relax and pulled her back down to him. 'Fair enough,' he conceded. 'I guess I'll just have to make pretty frequent trips down to Sydney and make sure I keep that highly active libido of yours under control.'

'You're... you're going to come down to Sydney to visit me?' she asked, glancing up again.

His eyes carried reproach, but his grin was very, very sexy. 'You don't think I'm going to let you get away from me as easily as that, do you?' He rolled her up and on to his chest. 'Of course I'm going to come down and visit you. Just as I expect you to visit me. I'm going to be your lover, woman, something I can't do by correspondence. Now kiss me, like a good girl. We haven't made love for at least an hour, and I'm getting mighty frisky again!'

CHAPTER NINE

BRYCE was all business the following morning, so much so that Adrianna began to wonder if the hot-blooded lover of the day before was a figment of her imagination. They breakfasted and broke camp soon after dawn, with Bryce saying that he wanted to be back at Dover Downs before the heat of the noonday sun.

They were making their way silently and steadily along an hour later, Adrianna having already seen signs of approaching civilisation with their frequent meeting of fences and gates, when she realised she still knew no real details about Bryce's life, his work, his family. She didn't even know his *age*!

She up-upped Dumbo till she drew level with Jumbo, bringing a questioning glance from Bryce. He looked marvellous this morning, she thought, distracted for a moment from her intention. Marvellous... Her eyes roved from his freshly shaven face down his broad chest to his hands and thighs, and she felt a tightening all over her body.

'Yes?' he prompted with a wicked twinkle in his bright blue eyes.

'Oh, I...I was thinking. I don't even know how old you are, or...or anything else about you.'

'*Now* she asks!' he drawled.

Her flush carried a small measure of guilt, and a bucketful of desire. 'Well? How old *are* you?'

'I turn thirty next month. Want to tell me how old you are?' he returned. 'Though I suspect twenty-seven or eight.' When she looked totally exasperated at his accuracy he laughed. 'Remember, you have told me quite a bit about yourself. I just added your college years on to a likely eighteen at leaving school, came up with twenty-four, then added two or three years for a hard-working, ambitious girl like you to make a success of her business.'

'I'm twenty-eight,' she admitted. 'Last May.'

'A Taurus?'

'Yes.'

'It figures,' was his wry comment.

'And what does *that* mean?' she bristled.

Bryce held up his hands in mock defence. 'Nothing, nothing. Taurus ladies are lovely, sweet, amenable females.' His smile was rueful. 'Once every hundred years or so.'

She went to hit him, but he grabbed her wrist and chuckled. 'Naughty, naughty! I can see I'm going to have fun with you, Adrianna. You're just like Bully. Unpredictable, wild...but a good mate, nevertheless!'

Her throat contracted as Bryce turned her palm over and lifted it to his mouth, his moist licking kiss sending hot shivers up and down her spine. But along with the physical pleasure was an appalled realisation of what Bryce had done to her. He had just said it, hadn't he? He *had* bonded her to him in the desert, like his dog. He had made her his pet, one that would grovel at his feet for a pat or a stroke, who would roll over on her back whenever he snapped his fingers. Even now she was quivering with need...

A surge of pride-filled anger and indignation had her wrenching her hand away. But he merely laughed and angled Jumbo closer, reaching over to cup the back of her head in a vice-like grip. 'That won't work any more, Adrianna. Not even remotely...' And with that he brought his face down to hers, giving her a brief but intimately possessive kiss. 'You see, my darling,' he husked, looking deeply into her eyes, 'you're mine, and there's nothing you can do about it, so stop trying, stop fighting it, stop going against everything that Mother Nature has ordained.' And he kissed her again.

But even as he evoked an inevitably fierce yearning in her there remained a deep core of rebellion that would not totally surrender to this man, *any* man. She jerked her head away and glared up at him. 'You can have my body, Bryce,' she said in a strangled voice, 'but that's where it ends!'

She was rocked by the glint of steely determination that burnt deep in those beautiful blue eyes. 'No, Adrianna,' he corrected strongly, 'that's where it *begins*!'

Then unexpectedly he flashed her a smile and urged Jumbo ahead, breaking the camels into a trot till another gate halted their progress. 'We're almost there now,' he announced quite happily, his manner seemingly unperturbed by their brief altercation. Adrianna was simply more confused than ever.

Suddenly the sound of an engine pricked up everyone's ears, especially Bully's. They all looked towards the horizon, the view unimpeded by the flat, sparsely treed countryside. A motorbike appeared, coming quickly, sending out a dusty cloud behind it. It was almost upon them by the time they had manoeuvred their way through the gate.

'It's Pete,' Bryce informed Adrianna, 'one of the stockmen on Dover Downs. He's probably on his way out to check the bores.'.

The noisy motorbike geared down to a rattling halt beside the well-behaved Jumbo, but Dumbo did his usual crabwards flight of nerves till the engine was cut dead.

'Hi, Pete,' Bryce called down to the grinning Aboriginal lad.

'Hi, boss. Back early?'

'Yep. Picked something up along the way that I needed to bring home.'

The cheeky black face moved across to Adrianna. 'Good-lookin' find, boss.'

'I reckon, Pete.'

'Gotta go, boss. That windmill in the far paddock wasn't workin' too well yesterday. Gotta fix it.'

'Want to take Bully with you?' Bryce suggested. 'You know how he likes riding on the back of the bike.'

'Sure thing, boss. Come on, dog.' Pete patted the seat behind him.

Bully gave a delighted bark and leapt on to the seat. 'See yuh, boss.' The motorbike roared off with Bully perched on the back like the Queen on a royal tour, his tail wagging a regal salute.

Adrianna didn't laugh as she might usually have done because she was busy giving Bryce a frowning look, a sick suspicion in the pit of her stomach. '*Boss*?' she directed at him, accusation in the word.

Bryce shrugged. 'I did try to tell you once.'

'You mean you *manage* Dover Downs?'

'Nope,' he smiled. 'I own it.'

'You . . . you own it?' she gulped.

''Fraid so.'

Her eyes narrowed. 'And just how large *is* Dover Downs?'

'Give or take an inch, about ten thousand square miles.'

She opened her mouth, then shut it again when a swear-word had been about to escape.

'Shall I say it for you?' teased Bryce, and leant over to whisper a vivid selection in her ear.

Adrianna pushed him away angrily. 'I think you *enjoyed* deceiving me!' she accused.

'You think so?'

'Yes!'

He gave another shrug. 'You could be right.'

'And what other surprises have you in store for me?'

'You'll just have to wait and see, won't you?'

'Oh, you . . .!'

'Temper, temper, Miss Taurus!'

Adrianna dragged in a steadying breath, determined she would not give him the satisfaction of being surprised or shocked by another single thing!

Which wasn't easy when she came face to face with an airstrip and hangars that boasted several helicopters and a luxurious twin-engined Beech Baron, not to mention the enormous colonial homestead perched on a hill overlooking a river, or the elegant woman in the blue sun-dress who came down from the house to the bottom of the hill to greet them, looking as if she'd just stepped out of an air-conditioned beauty salon.

'My mother,' Bryce murmured as the other woman approached.

She didn't look at all as she would have pictured his mother, Adrianna thought. Her own mother had become shapeless and worn over the years, but this woman was slim and smart, her face showing only a minimum of wrinkles.

'Bryce dear, what are you doing back so soon?' Blue eyes the same as Bryce's peered around at where

Dumbo had naturally ducked in behind Jumbo. 'My goodness, and who have we here?'

Bryce had stopped the camels near a group of outbuildings where a flock of happy smiling Aboriginal children seemed to have materialised from nowhere, not to mention a couple of weatherbeaten stock-hands. Now all of them joined Mrs McLean in staring up at Adrianna with avid curiosity.

'This is Adrianna Winslow, Mother,' Bryce explained. 'An intrepid lady pilot whose Cessna crashed not far from where I was camping. She wasn't hurt, but I could hardly leave her in the middle of nowhere, could I?'

The woman gave Adrianna a surprisingly thorough scrutiny, then beamed up at her son. 'So you brought her home.'

'Yes,' Bryce beamed back at her, 'I brought her home.'

Adrianna just knew those smiles held some secret message between them, but quite frankly she was too rattled to even hazard a guess at what it might be. She sighed, her shoulders slumping wearily.

'I think your friend is tired, dear,' Mrs McLean pointed out.

'Yes,' drawled Bryce, 'I imagine she is.'

Adrianna rolled her eyes at his knowing look, but allowed him to help her down and lead her up the formidable path and steps and into the astonishing cool of the house. Her head shook ruefully as she took in the air-conditioning, the elegant foyer, the spacious rooms leading off the wide central hall. No wonder his mother had looked refreshed!

She was guided into an enormous and very formal sitting area which had a huge mahogany fireplace and elaborately curtained French windows overlooking a

wide verandah. The polished wooden floors were
dotted with Persian rugs and the sofas and chairs were
covered in a subtle green brocade. Gilt-framed oil
paintings and exquisite old photographs hung on the
richly papered walls. A crystal chandelier hung heavily
above. It could easily have been a room out of a so-
ciety family's mansion.

Adrianna looked around in total confusion. Why
had Bryce kept his wealth a secret? Why...particularly
after they had become lovers?

'I think Adrianna would like a shower and a change
of clothes, Mother. I would too, but first I'll contact
the authorities, let them know she's all right. Have
you been hearing anything about a small plane crash
on the news?'

'Now, Bryce, you know I don't listen to the news
when I visit here.'

Bryce nodded, and Adrianna wondered where his
mother usually lived. Obviously not out here on Dover
Downs. Such a big house, she thought, for only one
man.

As though her thought had conjured up another
person, a very attractive Aboriginal girl suddenly appeared in the doorway. 'It's time for tea, Mrs
McLean,' she said in a low, husky voice. 'Will the
lady want some as well?' she asked, spotting
Adrianna.

'Yes, Helen. And some sandwiches and cake. We
have a *couple* of hungry travellers here.'

'Hello, Helen,' Bryce said from where he was
standing, a hand on the curtains of one of the large
French windows.

The girl was startled. 'Oh...Mr McLean! I didn't
see you there.' She blushed very prettily, Adrianna
thought, and jealousy stabbed into her heart.

She looked over to find Bryce's eyes upon her, and her chin lifted defiantly. His answering smile unnerved her. What else was she going to find out about this man whom she had taken to her heart? If he thought she was going to share him he had another think coming!

'Make up a tray, Helen,' Bryce suggested. 'Miss Winslow will have it in her room.'

Helen turned and walked away, leaving Adrianna with a clear impression of long brown legs, lovely dark eyes and lush full breasts.

'Good idea,' Mrs McLean agreed. 'I'll show you to your room, Adrianna, then Bryce can tell me all about your adventure.' She led her back out into the hall, turning right towards the back of the house.

'Not that way, Mother,' Bryce called after them sharply. 'Put her in Brett's room.'

Adrianna saw the flicker of surprise in his mother's face, but the woman nodded and took Adrianna the other way. 'Bryce is right,' she said as they walked along. 'The guest wing's too lonely.'

'Who's Brett?' asked Adrianna.

'Bryce's younger brother. There's only the two of them. I didn't have any daughters, though I would have dearly loved one.'

'And Brett doesn't live at home any longer?'

'No. He runs the family's other cattle property, over in the Channel Country. It's called Lowland Downs. Here we are...' She stopped and opened a door on the right and Adrianna stepped into an enormous, decidedly mannish room with heavy dark furniture, a royal blue quilt on the bed and few fripperies. 'I hope this will be all right,' Mrs McLean said uncertainly. She walked over and pushed the curtains back from the French doors, then pointed to an adjoining door.

'The bathroom's in there, but I'm afraid you have to share it with Bryce. His room is on the other side.'

For a second Adrianna stiffened, disturbed that Bryce's intentions had been obvious to his mother. 'It's fine,' she said with an edgy smile. 'I mean, it won't really matter, since Bryce is going to fly me down to Sydney later this afternoon, anyway.'

'*Is* he?' The other woman frowned. 'I would have thought he'd have you stay the night and take you down tomorrow morning.'

Adrianna blushed fiercely. 'Oh . . .'

The woman's glance was sharp, then softened to one of gentle concern. 'You can talk it over with Bryce when he brings you your tray. Now I'll just get you some fresh towels, a nightie in case you need it and something else to wear. I have some things here that should fit you and shouldn't be too matronly.'

'You're very kind,' Adrianna murmured.

'My dear, I'm only too pleased to do what I can. You must have had a . . . trying experience.'

A lump was gathering in Adrianna's throat. 'Yes . . . yes, it's been difficult.'

'We'll talk later, perhaps.'

Adrianna nodded. 'Yes.'

Mrs McLean came back with two cream towels and a négligé set that looked suspiciously like a leftover from a honeymoon—all white silk and see-through lace. Adrianna wondered wryly if Bryce had his mother trained to aid and abet him in his seductions, though the other clothes she left were not at all provocative: a pair of loosely fitting pink cotton trousers and a pink and white striped top. She also thoughtfully supplied her empty-handed guest with a toothbrush and a pair of cotton briefs, both obviously new, still in their plastic packets.

Adrianna moved almost nervously into the bathroom, but was relieved to see she could lock both doors from inside. The bathroom was almost as masculine as the bedroom, with austere brown and white tiles and plain gold taps. Brown bath mats covered the floor and there were no pots of cosmetics or cans of hairspray in sight on the spacious vanity unit. There was, however, a hairbrush and comb in one drawer she could use, and the shelf in the shower had a couple of choices of shampoo and conditioner.

Adrianna luxuriated in a long hot shower, shampooing her hair till it squeaked with cleanliness and revelling in the feel of drying herself with the thick, fluffy towels. A glance in the large vanity mirror showed a tan such as she had never had before, and a blush crept up her neck when she realised she had acquired it frolicking naked all day at the gorge.

She swallowed as she once again remembered how submissive she had been to Bryce's demands. No, not submissive, she amended. Very co-operative would better describe her behaviour. It still had the power to amaze her, but she knew she would act the same way again, whenever Bryce wanted her to. Such was his sexual power over her.

It distressed her to think she had come to this, not much different from her mother. The only thing she could cling to was her determination not to marry the man, or have children by him. Her earlier waffling about having a baby was by now well and truly stifled. And yet... her eyes travelled around the room. The situation had changed somewhat, hadn't it? It wasn't as though Bryce was a poor man. Or lazy. Or mean...

What about unfaithful? her honest side inserted. Something had transpired between him and that Aboriginal girl—she was sure of it.

Adrianna's chest tightened. Her father had been a handsome man, almost as handsome as Bryce, with a manner not dissimilar, an easy line of patter and a sexy, laid-back charm that women had found irresistible. It hadn't taken him long after he married her mother to begin sampling all that was readily on offer. What guarantee did she have that Bryce would be any different?

None, my dear, the answer came back, as swift and sure as a boomerang. None.

She was a fool to be tempted into thinking of marriage. A fool! Besides, hadn't Bryce decided he didn't want to marry her anyway, that he was content with the role of lover?

But a lover could be unfaithful too, couldn't he?

This thought brought such distress to Adrianna that her hands were shaking as she pulled on the day clothes Bryce's mother had given her. She was back out in the bedroom and brushing her hair with harsh, vigorous strokes when there was a knock on the door.

It would be Bryce, she thought, stomach aflutter.

But it was only Helen, standing there with a tray, her handsome face lit by a pleasant smile. Any relief, however, was short-lived as Bryce came strolling down the hall, taking the tray from the girl and coming into the room. 'Thank you, Helen,' he said without a backward glance.

The girl closed the door quietly, and left.

Adrianna fidgeted with the hairbrush while Bryce placed the tray on top of a large chest of drawers and began pouring her tea. 'I can do that for myself,' she said curtly.

'So you can,' he smiled, putting the teapot down and walking across the room, where he sat down on the side of the huge double bed. It creaked under his weight. 'I forgot my days of being your lackey were over.'

His words and manner irritated her for some reason, which was silly really. In love or not, she wanted to maintain her role of independent, liberated woman, didn't she? 'Huh!' she snorted. 'You were only my lackey because you didn't think I could do anything properly!'

'True.'

'Must you always sound so smug?' she flung at him.

His eyebrows shot upwards, but she noticed that underneath his reaction he was eyeing her refreshed self with an admiring gaze. She spun away and poured her tea. 'Your mother says you expect me to stay the night,' she said abruptly, replacing the rattling teapot on the tray.

'I would have thought that only sensible. Besides, there's no real reason for you to hurry back today, is there? I've notified the police, who agreed to contact both your family and your business associates. I gave this phone number in case anyone wants to contact you personally.'

'I . . . I would like to ring my mother myself . . . and Alan,' Adrianna added with a surge of butterflies in her stomach.

Bryce's mouth tightened. 'If you must.' He stood up and moved slowly towards her. She practically shrank back into the wall as he reached for her, but he only cupped her chin. His eyes carried a dry amusement. 'It's one step forward and two steps backward with you, isn't it, my love?'

'I . . . I don't know what you mean,' she said huskily.

'Oh, yes, you do... You know darned well what I mean. But one day, Adrianna, you might get a shock and find out that your preconceived ideas about men don't always apply. Meanwhile, I won't let this hot-and-cold act of yours bother me any more, because it's just an act.' He bent to brush her lips with his own in a tantalising and totally unsatisfactory manner. 'Just an act,' he murmured.

Adrianna clamped her teeth down hard to stop herself from throwing her arms around his neck and dragging his mouth down on hers. Shame at the truth behind his statement brought resentment and anger, but enough common sense remained not to deny what he was saying. It would probably only lead to his setting out to prove to her she was a hypocrite. And the last thing she could cope with at that moment was Bryce reducing her to a quivering, mindless, wanting wreck. Neither was she going to be cowed by his knowledge of her weakness. Her eyes were bold and proud as she glared up at him.

'Have you slept with that girl?' she demanded.

He seemed startled by this abrupt change of tack. 'You mean Helen?' he frowned.

'Of course I mean Helen,' she snapped, colour in her cheeks.

His smile was slow and almost cruel. 'You expect me to answer that?'

'Yes!' she hissed.

'Let me just say that while I'm in your bed, my sweet, I certainly won't be in hers.'

His blunt answer rocked her into silence.

'Is that satisfactory?' he drawled.

'What if I asked you to get rid of her?'

'What if I asked you never to see Alan again?' he countered.

Her mouth fell open, then slowly closed. 'I...see...'

'I hope so,' Bryce ground out in the closest he had come to anger all day. 'There's a phone in the foyer,' he stabbed out. 'Feel free to use it as often and for as long as you like.'

'Alan?'

'Adrianna?' He sounded stunned. 'Is that you?'

'Yes... Haven't the police been in touch with you yet?'

'No, I've just arrived back from Alice Springs. But my God, Adrianna, where are you? Do you realise I've had search planes looking for you for *days*? Are you all right? What happened?'

'It...it's a long story,' she began.

'Then tell me it, dear heart. I want to hear it all!'

Adrianna winced at his loving address and launched into the same nervous, edited version she had just finished telling her equally relieved mother.

'...and so you see, Alan, I'm really all right. Mr McLean brought me back to his property—Dover Downs. I...I'll give you the phone number...'

Alan wrote it down.

'Oddly enough, Adrianna, I think I know that McLean fellow,' he said. 'Is his name Bryce?'

'Yes,' she admitted shakily, 'you do know him. He told me he'd met you a few years back.'

Alan laughed. 'That's a mild way to describe our encounter! He came storming into my office one day demanding that I let my secretary leave because he had a date with her, yet the girl had known full well she might have to work late that day. A very good-looking fellow, as I recall, but too hot-tempered for my liking. Quite a ladies' man too. My secretary was only one in a long line of young women to be squired around Sydney by the handsome young grazier come to town. There were plenty of broken hearts when he had to return home quite suddenly, believe me! Anyway, that hardly matters now. That was years ago, but it's a small world, isn't it?'

'Y-yes.' A ladies' man, Adrianna kept thinking. Just like her father...

'You sound very tired, Adrianna. When are you coming back to Sydney so that I can look after you?'

Oh, God, she thought wretchedly.

'Adrianna? Are you sure you're all right?'

'Yes,' she admitted.

'I know this probably isn't the time, but have you given any thought to that question I asked you?' Alan went on.

'Yes...'

He gave a slightly nervous laugh. 'I don't like the sound of that yes.'

'Alan, I...'

His sigh carried resignation. 'Funny, I really thought you were going to say yes. Well, that's torn it!' he finished irritably.

'Alan, please don't be upset with me,' she begged.

'I'm not upset with you, Adrianna,' he sighed. 'Look, when are you getting back?'

'I'll be flying down to Sydney tomorrow.'

'Do you want me to meet you at the airport?'

'Well, I'm not sure exactly when I'll be arriving,' she hedged, knowing that Bryce was sure to be with her and would insist on taking her home.

'What about dinner, then? Or will you be too tired?'

'Dinner will be fine,' she said. What she had to say to Alan really couldn't wait.

'Seven o'clock?'

'I'll be ready.'

'I'm so glad you're all right, Adrianna. I just knew you would be.'

'Did you?' she laughed weakly.

'Of course. You're indestructible, my dear girl. A veritable tiger when cornered.'

'Oh, dear, I sound horrible!'

'Never. You're delightful.'

An embarrassed blush came to her cheeks, and at that moment Bryce appeared in the doorway opposite the phone table and just looked at her, his expression hard.

'I... I must go, Alan,' she stammered. 'I'll see you tomorrow night.'

Bryce walked over and took the receiver from her hand and hung it up. 'What's all this about tomorrow night, Adrianna?' he said coldly.

She steadied her burst of nerves. 'I'm going out to dinner with Alan, to explain the situation.'

'*Are* you? What's wrong with telling him over the phone?'

'He deserves better than that, Bryce.'

'And what about me? What do I deserve? You do realise that I intended flying you back and staying the night with you.'

She stiffened. '*Did* you?'

'I did.'

'Then I suggest that next time you make plans that involve me, you consult me first. I don't take kindly to people organising my life for me.'

'I'm not people, Adrianna. I'm the man you happen to love.'

'That doesn't mean you can take me for granted, Bryce,' she retorted.

He gave her a long, considering look, then slowly nodded. 'Point taken.'

Adrianna was so astonished by this concession that she was lost for words.

Bryce surveyed her surprise with a lazy smile. 'See? I'm capable of appreciating the arrogance of my sex. And I'm very capable of changing. All you have to do is show me the way.'

'And have you changed since your days in Sydney, Bryce?' she asked, wary of any man who claimed he could change. 'Or are you still a ladies' man?'

His instant anger alarmed her, because it was so controlled. 'Carstairs didn't wait long to put the knife in, did he?' he said bitingly.

Adrianna felt flustered. 'It . . . it wasn't like that,' she said, almost regretting having mentioned it now.

'Go out to dinner with him,' he ground out. 'But I'll be there waiting up for you when you get back, and God help him if I find out he's tried anything!'

And with blazing eyes, he whirled around and stalked off, leaving her standing there, staring after him, her heart pounding. Much as Adrianna didn't like Bryce being possessive and distrusting of her, she couldn't help being thrilled that he appeared to care about her so violently.

She walked slowly back to her bedroom where she picked up the lace and silk négligé, fingering the transparent lace panels while her mind whirled with her ambivalent feelings. She pressed the silk to her cheek and wondered with a quickened pulse if Bryce would come to her bed that night.

Or whether she would be forced to go to his.

CHAPTER TEN

THE BEECH BARON touched down at Sydney's small-craft airport at Bankstown shortly after two the following afternoon, the flight having been long and, for Adrianna, a strain.

The night before had not gone as expected. She had fallen asleep in the afternoon, not waking till nine in the evening, when Mrs McLean had brought her some supper on another tray. They had talked for a while, with Adrianna finding the woman as intelligent and charming as her son. Apparently she had a house in Adelaide where she now lived, though she often stayed with her two sons at their respective properties, mostly when one of her boys wanted a break for a while, either going to the city or on the occasional overseas holiday.

Bryce, it seemed, always went walkabout to wind down after mustering was completed, so it was a set arrangement that she look after Dover Downs while he was away. When Adrianna expressed surprise that a woman could manage such a big property, Bryce's mother explained that she had always actively helped her husband when he was alive—he had been tragically killed by lightning while out riding nine years before—and was quite capable of taking over the reins whenever needed.

Bryce had finally interrupted their little tête-à-tête, with his mother withdrawing tactfully. But if Adrianna thought he was going to make love to her or spend the night with her she was sorely mistaken. After a token talk and a peck on the forehead he had said goodnight, saying he was very tired and wanted to get an early start the next day. Adrianna had lain in that big lonely bed until the early hours of the morning, tossing and turning, till finally she had succumbed to sheer emotional exhaustion.

The morning found her feeling edgy and strained. It bothered her that her future lay ahead of her as a series of restless, sleepless nights, all because of this awful state she had got herself into over Bryce. Falling in love with as self-destructive as she had always known it would be, she thought unhappily as she got up and stripped off, tossing the wasted négligé on to a chair in frustration.

Breakfast was a trial, with Bryce looking even more disgustingly attractive than ever, his crisply ironed short-sleeved shirt a dazzling white against his tan, and the tight, stone-washed jeans hugging his lean hips and muscular thighs like a second skin.

Adrianna did her best to act naturally, but underneath she was annoyed with him, especially when he kept flashing a blushing Helen those sexy smiles of his. Jealousy was an emotion Adrianna was not used to, or comfortable with. It underlined the way love affected one's life—and not for the better!

It was a partial relief that his mother accompanied them to the airstrip, and that two of the stockmen wanted a ride to Sydney for their yearly holidays, as their presence prevented any intimate conversation between herself and Bryce. Adrianna needed time to get her shrewish thoughts under control.

But as soon as Bryce had her alone in the hire car he had organised to be waiting at the airport for him, he gave voice to her suspicion that she had been making her feelings all too obvious.

'Like to tell me what's eating you?' he demanded.

'Nothing,' she grumped. 'I just don't feel like talking.'

'Suits me,' he shrugged, and fell silent.

This irritating refusal to give her raw nerves the balm of a good argument annoyed Adrianna all the more. She sat there in a brooding silence, watching through the side window while Bryce manoeuvred the nifty Saab through the traffic in the direction of the city, taking back streets and short-cuts with the sureness and expertise of a taxi-driver. It piqued her that she had felt like a fish out of water in the outback, whereas Bryce was as much at home in the city as she was.

'And just how much time *have* you spent in Sydney?' she finally burst out.

He gave her a narrow-eyed look. 'Spit it out, sweetheart. You've been wanting to since you got up this morning. And it's certainly got nothing to do with my knowing where I'm going. Which, at the moment,' he added cryptically, 'I'm not sure I really do!'

Adrianna found his comment confusing. Bryce never seemed unsure of anything. It was she who was always confused, bewildered, disorientated these days. Here she was about to begin a chapter in her life she had no blueprints for, and she didn't know what to do, how to act. With Alan she had always been sure.

'Just tell me *why* you didn't stay with me last night?' she asked wretchedly. 'Why you didn't want to make love to me?'

His eyes showed true astonishment. 'Is that what this is all about? My not spending the night with you?' His laughter was relieved and happy. 'My God, Adrianna, I thought I was doing the right thing! I thought I was being considerate—my mother said you looked tired. I can't win with you, can I? Hell, I paced up and down the room into the early hours for nothing!'

He threw her a smouldering look that allayed any fears she had that he had grown tired of her already.

'Oh, Bryce,' she cried, 'I . . . I thought you might not want me any more!'

'Just point me in the direction of your unit, my love,' he growled, 'and I'll show precisely how much I want you.'

Adrianna's heartbeat revved up with the car, and by the time she directed Bryce into her allotted car-space under her block of units she was in a high state of excitement. They made their way swiftly to the es-calator that would take them up to the tenth floor and her unit. Side by side and silent, they stood together in the lift, the sexual tension between them con-suming Adrianna with a wave of hot awareness, making the small space encompassing them seem even smaller, and suffocatingly intimate. She was thinking of holding his hand when the doors whooshed open and camera flashlights began popping off in her face, journalists with notepads pushing forward.

'Miss Winslow, tell us about the crash!'

'Miss Winslow, did you know that your plane was hit by a piece of space debris falling to earth?'

'How does it feel to find yourself lost in the middle of the desert, Miss Winslow?'

'What about the man that rescued you, Miss Winslow? A Mr McLean, wasn't it? I hear you spent some considerable time alone in the outback with him?'

Luckily enough they didn't appear to know that the man with her was the aforementioned Mr McLean. If they did he would have been besieged with ques-

tions as well. As it was, after the initial shock,
Adrianna handled the situation without too much
trouble, telling the media with a firm no-nonsense approach that she was exhausted, that she wanted no
publicity other than the report given to the police,
and that if they harassed her further the same police
would be called and if they didn't leave she would
have her bodyguard—this, indicating Bryce with a curt
nod—remove them forcibly from the premises.

'Bodyguard?' Bryce repeated wryly once the unit
door was closed and locked.

Adrianna noticed for the first time that he was
looking peeved. He was also glancing around the
smartly furnished unit with a gathering frown as
though he didn't like being actually confronted with
the evidence of her material success. She could understand his feelings only too well. Being confronted by
his wealth had been a none too pleasant shock, for it
underlined all she didn't know about him, and made
a mockery of what she had believed him to be.

Still, she had never hidden her background from
him, which made his frowning a puzzle. The feeling
that he was withdrawing from her brought true alarm.
In the lift they had seemed so close to each other,
their mutual desire overriding any other doubts they
had. Adrianna refused to let them crowd back, refused to let them spoil what she wanted most at that
moment.

Moving quickly to him, she slid her arms up over
the hard wall of his broad chest and around his strong
neck. 'And a very good bodyguard you'd make too,'
she murmured seductively.

But when she went to go up on tiptoe and kiss him,
he pulled back.

She stared up at him. 'What's wrong?'

'Most men like to make the first move, Adrianna,' he rebuked.

'But that's silly and old-fashioned,' she said softly, and pressed herself closer. 'I want to make love to you, Bryce...the way I did out at the gorge. Please let me...'

He groaned, and bent his lips to hers with a primitive hunger that took her by surprise, ravaging her mouth with an intensity bordering on violence, his tongue plunging deep, his hands bruising on her back. Then with a single savage movement he tore his mouth from hers, swept her up into his arms and carried her into the bedroom.

Adrianna woke with a long satisfied sigh, her mind filling with erotic memories: Bryce, stripping her quite roughly; semi-brutal hands moving over her naked flesh in an incredibly arousing fashion; their ultimate and very exhausting union.

A large arm slid under her shoulders and pulled her back into him, spoon-fashion. 'You called?' he whispered, his lips feathering over her ear.

A shiver rippled down her spine and her eyes shot open, making her suddenly aware that there was very little light coming through the bedroom curtains. She sat up abruptly, snapping on the bedside lamp. Her bedside clock showed ten past six. 'Heavens, look at the time! I'd better go and shower and get dressed. Alan said he'd be here at seven, and he's never late.'

'God forbid,' Bryce mocked drily from where he was lying on the bed, his arms tucked behind his head, a sheet half covering his body.

Adrianna got up and walked naked over to the small walk-in wardrobe, where she slipped into her silk kimono, returning to the bedroom to give Bryce a frowning look. 'Why exactly are you so antagonistic towards Alan? Surely you can't still be harbouring a grudge over something that happened years ago? Besides, I think you were hasty in your judgement of him back then. It couldn't have been easy having to run a business at his young age. And it's not as though that secretary was the only young woman in your life. You seem to have been a very busy lad in the romance department!'

Adrianna hadn't meant to put in that last little dig, but once it was said, she refused to back down. She had been wanting to ask Bryce about his time in Sydney for ages.

Bryce's returning look was narrow-eyed and angry. He propped himself up on one elbow and glared at her. 'You're very quick to hop to Carstairs' defence, aren't you? *And* to understand him. How about a bit of understanding for me as well, eh? I was only young too. Barely turned twenty, with a country upbringing that undoubtedly put me years behind my city counterparts. One look at Alan Carstairs told me just how far!'

He made a scoffing sound. 'And believe me, he was running his father's business with an efficiency and ruthlessness that was awesome!'

He tossed back the sheet and sat up, swinging his bare legs over the side of the bed. 'You want to know what I've got against Carstairs besides the obvious?' he growled. 'I'll tell you. It's memories, Adrianna. Memories of a time I'd rather forget, memories of a boy who selfishly wanted to rebel against everything he'd been brought up to be, and a father who was big enough to let him go for a while, even though it probably cost him his life!'

Adrianna's heart turned over as she saw Bryce's shoulders slump and his face grow bleak. He looked so down she came forward and sat beside him placing a comforting hand on his shoulders. 'It wasn't your fault, darling,' she said softly. 'Your mother told me about it. It was an accident...'

His eyes were pained as they met hers. 'Maybe... But I can't help feeling that I should have been there, helping him, not gallivanting around in the city, acting like some adolescent idiot, chasing every bit of skirt that came my way. Poor Dad, I let him down...'

'No, you didn't,' she soothed, replacing her hand with soft lips. 'As you said, you were only a boy. Don't be so hard on yourself...' And of course he *had* been only a boy at the time.

He reached out and curved a gentle hand around her cheek. 'You *do* understand, don't you?' he said. His kiss was warm and tender as he tipped her back across the bed. The hand on her cheek slid down her throat then inside the robe, caressing her breast with light, stroking movements.

'Oh, Bryce!' she moaned, her need for him intense and instant.

He stopped kissing her mouth and pressed his lips to her throat. 'Don't go out to dinner with Carstairs,' he whispered. 'Put him off... Call him.'

Adrianna froze.

The hand on her breast did likewise.

He withdrew it with a sigh and she got up, retying her robe with shaking hands. The thought that Bryce had just tried to manipulate her through sex was churning away inside her as she turned on him. 'Don't you ever do that to me again,' she blazed. '*Ever!*'

'Do what?' he said in a flat, tired voice.

'Try to get your own way by...by... Damn it, Bryce!' She stamped her foot. 'You *know* what I'm talking about!'

Bryce sighed again and leant over to where his clothes were scattered beside the bed. He dressed with remarkable speed, and when he began to walk from the bedroom, Adrianna ran after him, catching at his arm. 'What...where are you going?'

'Home,' was his curt reply.

'But...but...'

His jaw clenched down hard. 'I wasn't trying to manipulate you, Adrianna. Not in the way *you* meant. And if you think I'm going to stay here and watch you doll yourself up to go out with that man, then you must be crazy!'

She blinked up at him, unable to take in this unexpected development quickly enough to know what to say.

'Look,' Bryce ground out, 'I always said I wouldn't play sophisticated games, but that's not strictly true, Adrianna. I have been playing a game. A desperate one.'

'A...a game?' she repeated weakly.

'That's right. I've been pretending I didn't want to marry you. Insane as it is, I *do*. I thought, if I gave you some time, you would eventually come round to my way of thinking. I had some sort of crazy idea, you see, that this problem of yours was a temporary hangover from your upbringing. She'll get over it, I kept telling myself. She'll see I'm not anything like her father. But now I'm not so sure. I don't think you will change, Adrianna—your distrust of men and their motives goes too deep. So I think the best thing I can do is get out of here while I still can!'

When he went to move she clung on tightly, frantically. 'But you can't go, Bryce. You can't!'

'Too damned right I can,' he returned hotly. 'And
I'm warning you, don't come after me unless you've
changed your mind about marrying me and having
my children!' And with that, he walked out, slamming
the door behind him.

Adrianna stared at the door for ages, unable to
think or move. But then she began to pace up and
down, up and down, her emotions churning, her mind
arguing frantically with her heart.

Let him go, common sense kept saying. You knew
it was hopeless. *Hopeless*! He wants too much.
Expects too much! If you marry him you'll be
wretched . . . miserable.

But I'm miserable *now*, her heart cried.

So what? a cynical voice shot back. You'll get over
it. In time . . . So will Bryce. And a damned sight
quicker than you, my dear. How long do you think
it'll be before he hops into the easy comfort of Helen's
bed, eh? Leopards don't change their spots. Once a
ladies' man, always a ladies' man!

Adrianna's heart hit rock bottom as this last truth
hit home.

She stopped pacing and threw herself down on the
sofa, tears flooding into her eyes. The sound of the
doorbell ringing made her jump to her feet, her eyes
blinking madly. He's come back, was her immediate
thought, and against all reason her heart soared. The
tears were dashed away as she flew to wrench open
the door, her face full of wild hope and happiness.

Alan stood on the doorstep, his smoky blue eyes
showing surprise as they took in her wide-eyed
expression. He frowned at her state of undress and

glanced at his watch. 'It *was* seven we agreed on, wasn't it?'

Adrianna face fell and she did the only possible thing. She burst into tears.

Alan, in true gentlemanly fashion, strode inside, closed the door, then gathered her weeping frame against his elegant grey suit. 'There, there, my love,' he soothed, stroking her hair. 'Was it that bad out in the desert? There, there... It'll be all right now. I'm here...'

She pulled away from his embrace, tears streaming down her face, despair making her strike out blindly. 'No, no, that's not it at all! Don't you see? You can't make anything right. Bryce is the only one who can do that,' she went on in choked, broken words. 'I love him... and need him, and... and he does love me... I think. He wants me to marry him, but I won't... I can't! So he left me and... and... Oh, God,' she sobbed, 'I can't live without him!'

To give Alan credit, he reacted to her muddled outburst with a remarkable degree of composure, though there was a definite tightening of muscles along his jawline. 'Ah, now I see! Our Mr McLean did a little more than just rescue you, didn't he?'

Adrianna slumped down on the sofa, her head dropping into her hands. 'Oh, Alan,' she groaned, 'I'm so sorry. I didn't mean to blurt it out like that.'

He laid a heavy hand on her shoulder. 'Never mind, my love. Never mind. We all make fools of ourselves over matters of the flesh. Believe me, I know.'

The pained undercurrent in his words had Adrianna lifting her soggy lashes and looking up at him. 'You've been in love too, Alan?'

His eyes betrayed true pain before he turned to stride across the room to the drinks cabinet. 'I'll get you a gin and tonic,' he muttered. 'You look as if you could do with one. I certainly could. Though I think I'll skip the tonic.' He went about it with his usual efficiency, stalking out to the kitchen to get some ice, then returning to hand over her glass and sink down in one of the roomy armchairs, his face bleak.

'In love, you ask?' His sigh was weary. 'It's hard to believe one falls truly in love with an eighteen-year-old girl. It's more likely lust.'

Now it was Adrianna's turn to stare. 'You mean...'

'My ward. Yes—Ebony.' His face twisted into a grimace and he took a hefty swig of straight gin. 'I don't understand it. For three years she's been flitting in and out of my life, a quiet little thing who hardly ever said boo to a grasshopper. Then last holidays Mother threw her an eighteenth birthday party and she came out all dressed up in this white lace dress, and immediately all I wanted to do was...' He shuddered.

'...make love to her?' Adrianna finished softly.

'What a delicate way of putting it!' was his black remark. 'Unfortunately I rarely feel delicate when I look at her these days.'

They both fell silent for a few seconds. Adrianna's mind was a merry-go-round of thoughts till one single realisation overrode all the others. 'Alan, is this the reason you asked me to marry you?'

His sigh was ragged. 'Yes. She finishes school in a month. She'll be in my home permanently from then on. I thought...'

'...that there'd be less danger for the girl if you had a wife by your side,' she finished gently.

'Yes,' he confessed.

An awkward silence fell between them till Alan spoke up again. 'I'm sorry, Adrianna, truly sorry. I didn't think of it as using you. You're my dearest friend. I guess I'm used to turning to you in my hours of need. Remember the night we first made love?'

'Yes,' she said warily.

'It was not long after Ebony's parents' funeral. I felt ... distraught when I saw those two coffins being lowered into the ground. Distraught and ... lonely. For years I'd done nothing but work, with few outside interests. My personal life had deteriorated into a night here and there with women I barely knew. Suddenly I wanted ... no, *needed* ... something more. Something decent and warm and special. You gave me that something, Adrianna, and for that I'll be eternally grateful. I'll never regret our relationship. I hope you won't either.'

She looked at him then and saw that he was very sincere in what he said. 'Oh, Alan, why couldn't I have fallen in love with you, instead of some crazy outback man?'

He gave a short, dry laugh. 'I might say the same, my love. Why couldn't I have fallen in love with you, instead of...' He broke off abruptly as he realised what he was saying. A dark frown bunched his brows together and he glared down into his drink. 'Must be the gin,' he muttered, and drained the rest.

Adrianna frowned as she sipped her drink. She knew Alan, and she knew the type of person he was. Much the same sort of man as she was a woman—serious, hardworking. Certainly not sex-mad. If he felt such strong physical feelings for the girl there was sure to be more to it than lust, just as in her case with Bryce.

'I think you're mistaken, Alan,' she argued quietly. 'I think you do love Ebony, but your desire for her is so strong that it overwhelms these deeper, finer

feelings. I know what I'm talking about, because that
was what I thought I was feeling for Bryce till I realised how much I liked and admired him as well.
Love can be a very deceiving emotion. It plays tricks
on us because sometimes we're frightened of love,
frightened of the risks it entails.'

She hesitated then, her heart turning over with
dismay at what she had just said. Who was she to talk
about risk-taking? She wasn't prepared to take any,
was she? She claimed to like and admire Bryce.
Claimed to actually *love* the man! But the basic truth
was she didn't have the courage to put that love on
the line . . .

She lifted the gin and tonic to her lips and gulped
down a mouthful, only to find Alan staring at her
when she lowered the glass.

'You've changed, Adrianna,' he said slowly.
'You've discovered passion. I almost envy Bryce
McLean.'

The irony of his statement dragged at her heart.
She stared down into her glass and swirled the re-
mainder of the drink in circles. 'I wouldn't if I were
you. I'm bad news for any man.'

'I don't agree. You have qualities a lot of men would
kill for. Why don't you go after him?' Alan urged.
'Find some way to make it work. If anyone can, you
can. You can be very determined, Adrianna, when
you want to be.'

For a second his words sent a surge of hope into
her heart. Did she dare do as he suggested? Was there
some sort of compromise acceptable to both Bryce
and herself? But then her heart sank. If there was she
couldn't think of it. Bryce was a black and white man,
a man who, once he had an idea fixed in his mind,

could not be swayed from it. Just look at the way he
still disliked Alan after all these years!

A thought popped into Adrianna's head and her
eyes snapped up to Alan's. 'Would you mind if I asked
you a highly irrelevant question?'

He raised a single eyebrow in mild surprise. 'Such
as?'

'Why didn't you go to your father's funeral?'

He stared at her. 'That *is* an odd question!' But
then the penny dropped. 'Ah, I think I get the
picture... McLean never did like me much. Neither
did my secretary.' His smile was rueful. 'Believe me,
I wanted to go to Dad's funeral, and if I could go
back in time, I would do so. But at twenty-one, I
didn't have the confidence to tell the bank to get
stuffed.'

'The bank?' Adrianna repeated, puzzled.

'The bank who held the mortgages on the family
home and business. They insisted on sending one of
their auditors over that day to inspect the books and
the business. They didn't believe I could pull it out
of the mire of debt my father had run up in the years
before he became ill. I couldn't see any way out of
the appointment, so the funeral went ahead without
me, though I held my own private service later that
evening. I really wasn't the heartless bastard back in
those days that I seemed to be. Just a young man
under a lot of stress. Does that restore me in your
eyes a little?'

'You never did need restoring in my eyes!' she assured him.

'Not even now,' he said slowly, 'that you know
about Ebony?'

Adrianna's heart contracted slightly, but she kept
a straight face. 'Not even now. As you said, Alan,

we're friends. And friends understand and forgive each other.'

Alan smiled. 'OK, friend. Then might I make a suggestion?'

'Of course.'

'I gather going out to dinner is off, but why don't you go and put some clothes on and I'll have some food sent up. You look as if you could do with some sustenance.'

Adrianna stood up, then hesitated. 'Alan, you do realise that there can never be any more... physical intimacy between us, don't you?'

Again his smile was gentle. 'Naturally. You're in love, and I know you'd never betray that love. I would never ask you to.'

Adrianna turned then and walked into the bathroom, a frown coming to her face. But aren't I betraying it right now? she worried. Didn't I betray it the moment I let Bryce walk out of here and out of my life so easily, the moment I chose not to go after him?

You can still go after him, an inner voice intervened. Of course, it will mean giving up everything you hold dear, everything you've ever worked for...

Instinctively she recoiled at the thought. I can't, she shuddered. I just can't!

CHAPTER ELEVEN

ADRIANNA circled the chartered Cessna over Dover Downs several times before setting the plane down on the private airstrip with only a few light bumps, then taxiing down to the hangars. She switched off the engine with a ragged sigh, only then admitting to herself that the flight—and the landing—had been almost as harrowing as the days leading up to it.

It hadn't occurred to her that she would be so nervous behind the controls of a plane—her previous accident had hardly been her fault, after all—but her heart had been in her mouth from the moment she had taken off from Darwin airport and she was very relieved to be safely on the ground.

Which brought her to another problem. The hangars looked deserted, no one coming out to see who had just arrived. She had thought someone would be there who could drive her up to the main house, but not a soul was in sight. She pushed open the door of the cockpit and the blistering heat hit her in the face.

'Just as well I wore light clothing,' she muttered, looking down at her ice lemon sundress and low-heeled white sandals. It would be a long, hot walk up to the house.

It was then that she spotted the approaching cloud of dust, preceded by a light blue Utility.

Would it be Bryce at the wheel? she wondered. The thought brought a surge of adrenalin and nerves.

She had never intended to come. After Bryce had left her she had finally and irrevocably decided that she would try to forget him, try to put him out of her heart and her mind.

She might as well have told herself not to breathe.

Still, it had taken her ten full days to give in, ten days of agonising and waffling and worrying, ten days of heartache and loneliness and frustration.

The arrival of her period a couple of days after Bryce left had made her oddly depressed, though it was only to be expected, and she had tried to get on with her life as usual, tried to find distraction in working.

But it had been useless. Most days she had merely stared at blank pages, her mind devoid of creative urges, though she should have been getting on with next year's winter designs.

How many times did she find herself reaching for the telephone to ring Bryce? Once she actually dialled his number, which she'd found out from Information, only to hang up before anyone had time to answer. Her hands had begun to shake uncontrollably, and what would she have said anyway? I love you, Bryce? I miss you, but I still can't live the sort of life you want me to? What would that have achieved?

So the calls had never been made.

Everyone in the office had commented how tired and strained she was looking and suggested she have some time off. They had all said they could cope without her for a while, which she didn't doubt at all. It seemed everything had swung along quite sweetly during her missing days in the desert, with her assistants making any necessary business decisions for her. Adrianna had always hired the very best. And the best were always waiting their chance to show what they could do.

In the end she had to admit that she couldn't go on as she was, going through the motions without energy or enthusiasm. Being away from Bryce and his loving had taken all the joy out of living. What did it matter if she had to give up her career? If she went on the way she was, soon she wouldn't have a career to give up!

Yet even then she hadn't been able to call him on the telephone. Perhaps she was half afraid he wouldn't talk to her, that he would still be angry. Whatever the reason, she felt it better if she just came and confronted him, told him she had changed her mind, that she did want to marry him, even though she still had her doubts about their long-term happiness. It wasn't the thought of children that frightened her so much now, but the sort of life Bryce would expect her to lead as his wife. And of course there was still that niggling little doubt that he might not be the most constant husband in the world. That was one thing Adrianna didn't think she could live with.

But perhaps she was wrong about that. Perhaps, like Alan, he had changed since those early days. Hadn't he claimed at Dover Downs that day that he could change, that she only had to show him the way? She hoped so. Anyway, all she could do was explain her doubts and fears to Bryce, and then it was up to him, wasn't it?

Yet now that the moment was at hand she was attacked by different doubts. He hadn't telephoned her, had he? He hadn't written either. He had, to all intents and purposes, wiped her from his life. Maybe she was wasting her time. Maybe he wouldn't want any more to do with her.

She climbed down from the cockpit, carrying the overnight bag she had packed when she'd been more optimistic, and walked with growing apprehension over to where the utility had pulled up at the edge of the tarmac. Because of its dusty windscreen she couldn't see who was at the wheel till she drew level with the passenger window.

A sigh of relief fluttered from her lips when she saw Mrs McLean sitting there in a pretty floral dress, beaming at her. 'Get in!' Bryce's mother called. 'I've kept the air-conditioning going for you.'

Adrianna quickly settled herself and her bag in the cool cabin. 'Thanks for coming down to meet me,' she said.

'No trouble. We always meet any plane that lands. Bryce is out in the far paddocks checking fences, I'm afraid. He won't be back for another hour or two.'

Adrianna gave the other woman a close look. How much did she know? she wondered. 'Has...has Bryce spoken to you about what happened between him and me?' she asked carefully.

'In what way?' The woman frowned.

'The day he flew me home to Sydney...we had a...a difference of opinion.'

'I see... That explains it, then.'

'Explains what?'

'Bryce's mood. He hasn't exactly been his bright breezy self this last week. I thought he was just missing you. He didn't say you'd argued or anything.'

Adrianna felt a surge of hope. So Bryce had been miserable too, had he? Clearly he hadn't been able to dismiss her from his life any more easily than she had been able to forget him. Though his moodiness could have been due to damaged ego. Or sexual frustration. 'Do you think he'll be pleased to see me?' she asked.

Mrs McLean's hesitation betrayed reservation at this. 'He doesn't usually like to be caught at a disadvantage,' she said by way of an answer. But then she smiled. 'Still, he's not likely to stay angry with the woman he loves for long.'

Adrianna's heart jumped. 'He *told* you he loved me?'

'He didn't have to. A mother knows when her son is in love. I knew it the moment he brought you home.'

'Oh!'

Her laugh was gentle as she put the Utility into gear. 'I always used to tease Bryce that he never brought a girl home for me to meet. He told me quite firmly that when and if he brought a girl home it would be the one he wanted to marry.'

Adrianna's heart turned over. So that was what Bryce and his mother had been smiling at that day!

Mrs McLean swung the Utility round and began heading along the rough road that led past the outbuildings back towards the main house.

Adrianna sighed.

It brought a sharp look. 'Don't you want to marry my son?'

She gave the other woman a pleading glance. 'I have to be honest with you. At first I didn't. I didn't think marriage was what I wanted at all.'

'But Bryce *has* asked you to marry him?'

'Well, yes . . . but . . .'

'You make it sound as if marrying Bryce is something to be wary of,' the other woman said indignantly. 'I'll have you know that he's a splendid man— simply splendid. And I'm not speaking through the blind eyes of a mother. Ask any of the cattlemen. Ask *anyone* around here! Oh, he went through some unsettled years when he thought he didn't want to even *see* another cow, let alone work with them. Went to Sydney to have a taste of the bright lights for a while. His father let him go, said it was good for him to see how the other half lived, give him a better basis to judge for himself what was right or wrong for him. When his father was killed, he came back like a shot to take his rightful position as head of the family. Not grudgingly either. He's told me many a time how much he's learned to value life on the land. Not that it's an easy life...'

She flashed Adrianna a narrow-eyed look. 'Is that what's been bothering you? The life you'd have to live if you married Bryce?'

'Partly,' she admitted.

'Humph! I wouldn't have taken you for a cowardly girl. OK, so it requires some sacrifices, but it's not as though you'd be poor. And since you can fly a plane, you could come and go to the city as often as you liked. There isn't anything Bryce wouldn't do for the woman he loved. You wouldn't even have to give up that business of yours. Though surely some of the creative work could be done from here, couldn't it?'

Adrianna just stared at Mrs McLean. Now why hadn't she thought of that? A burst of joy gushed through her. Even her earlier creative block disappeared, images from her days in the outback jumping into her mind with inspired flashes. She would start a special range of outback designs, using fabrics that reflected the strong colours she had seen for herself—the red of the sand, the bronzes and yellow ochres of the rocks, the bright blue of the sky and the deep green of the gorge. And then there was the black and orange of the cockatoos. The styles would be light and cool, loosely fitting and comfortable. Oh, her ideas were endless!

'Of course things might change when the kiddies come along,' the woman was saying, snapping Adrianna back from her flights of fancy to the reality of life. 'You might have to stay at home a bit more then, but even in that you wouldn't be alone. You have *me*, you know. I'm as fit as a fiddle. I'd come and babysit my grandchildren as often as you'd like.'

Adrianna was startled by this generous offer at first, but then she sighed and nodded. How silly she had been to think that all mothering was like the one experience she had been involved in! Most families were only too happy to share the workload, making the inevitable stresses and pressures of looking after children not only bearable, but probably enjoyable.

'And then there's Helen,' Bryce's mother went on. 'She's a good one with children, as are all the Aboriginal women who live at Dover Downs. Though I dare say Helen will have a baby of her own soon, since she's marrying Pete next month.'

'Helen's getting married?' Adrianna gasped.

'And none too soon, I'd say,' the other woman sniffed. 'She's been impossible since she fell in love, going round giggling and blushing all the time.'

'Then there's nothing between...' Adrianna's voice broke off before she could give voice to her jealous fears. A wry smile captured her mouth. Bryce had deliberately baited her with Helen. She could see it all so clearly now. His smiles had been no more than a ploy to make her jealous. And how well they had succeeded!

'Does that smile mean you've made up your mind?'

Adrianna glanced over at Bryce's mother, her smile widening. 'If he'll have me.'

Mrs McLean grinned back. 'If he doesn't I'll skin him alive!'

Adrianna settled back in the seat, feeling definitely happier, but not nearly as smug as Bryce's mother. It was all very well for the two women who loved Bryce to talk about him and settle his life for him. But would the man himself have the same ideas?

CHAPTER TWELVE

BRYCE swept into the house shortly after two-thirty and made straight for his bedroom, unaware that Adrianna was sitting in the kitchen, nervously awaiting his arrival. She had been keeping Helen company while Mrs McLean had an afternoon nap, and had found the girl quite delightful once she was past her shyness.

'That's Mr McLean now,' Helen said when she heard the front door bang. 'He always showers first, then goes into his study for the rest of the afternoon.'

'Do you take him coffee or tea or anything?' Adrianna asked, trying to think of some excuse to go to him quite naturally.

Helen shook her head. 'No, he usually has a beer. There's a small refrigerator in his study.'

'Oh...'

'Why don't you wait for him in there anyway? Unless you'd like to go along to his bedroom?' At this Helen giggled and blushed.

Adrianna smiled. 'No, his study will do. Show me the way, will you?'

It was another very masculine room with a polished parquet floor and wood-panelled walls, the furnishings in autumn tones. A large heavy desk sat on a rust-toned rug between the two long windows that faced the outside, a rich brown leather chair behind it, two armchairs in front—one a darker brown, the other a mustard gold. A modern personal computer sat on one end of the desk, a fax machine on the other, both looking incongruous in the old-style décor.

Adrianna spent her time waiting for Bryce inspecting the various books in the sturdy Victorian bookcases. There were a lot on cattle and cattle management and several on modern computerised bookkeeping. Clearly Bryce was not a man to fall behind the times.

She was standing at one of the windows, staring out at the hot, dry landscape, feeling sick with nerves, when the door opened abruptly. Bryce didn't see her till he went to close the door. His hand froze on the knob and he just stood there, staring at her.

Adrianna did a bit of staring herself, for Bryce wasn't wearing all that much. Just a pair of white shorts and a white, short-sleeved shirt open to the waist.

'Adrianna!' he breathed.

'Bryce . . .' Her taut face broke into an encouraging smile.

She saw his hand tighten where it still held the doorknob. His eyes hardened as they travelled slowly down her body, then back up again.

Oh, God, she thought. He doesn't want me any more.

She cleared her throat. 'Bryce, I . . .'

He clenched his jaw even harder and swung the door shut. 'What are you doing here, Adrianna?' he grated. 'Believe me when I say you will *not* be allowed to toy with my feelings again!' He strode over to the desk, where he snatched up a pile of mail and began sorting through the letters, not giving her another glance.

Despair was like a dagger in Adrianna's heart. She was too late.

No, she refused to think that! She loved Bryce and wanted him. She hadn't come all this way to give up now.

'I wouldn't do that, Bryce,' she tried to assure him, but her voice shook uncontrollably. 'I . . . I love you.'

The blue eyes were chilling as they lifted to hers. 'Is that so? And what, may I ask, does that mean? What does it entitle me to expect? An adoring little woman prepared to lay her life at my feet?'

Adrianna couldn't help her automatic cringe.

His mouth twisted cruelly at her reaction to his words. 'I didn't think so,' he scoffed. 'Playing the sweet submissive wife isn't in your line, is it? So where does that leave us? What, I ask myself, is behind this mission of *love*! Could it be. . .?' His gaze flicked over her body once more. 'Ah, yes . . . How silly of me not to realise that your visit might have an extremely basic aim.'

He put down the letters and began walking around the desk towards her, his face hard, his gaze mocking. 'I have to give you credit, my sweet—you've come well armed. I mean . . . have you got *any* underwear on at all? I can't see any bra or stockings. No petticoat either. The sunlight shining through the window is like an X-ray on that dress. That doesn't leave much, does it?'

He stopped in front of her and ran a contemptuous fingertip around the low square neckline of her dress, making her shiver. 'This is why you've come, isn't it?' he snarled, his hands sliding slowly down the sides of her dress, then moving back up, taking the skirt with them.

Adrianna couldn't seem to get her mind into gear, shock and excitement warring a fierce battle inside her. Stop him! her pride screamed.

She staggered backwards against the curtains, her eyes wide, her throat swallowing convulsively. 'No,' she denied shakily, 'it's not why I've come.'

His laugh was scornful. 'You *don't* want me to make love to you?'

Her face showed total dismay at his derision. 'Of course I want you to make love to me. But not like this... Not with you sneering at me and thinking I'm some sort of...of...My God, Bryce, didn't you mean what you said before you left?' she cried. 'Don't you love me any more?'

'Oh, yes, I meant what I said before I left,' he jeered. 'And I still love you, more's the pity! But have *you* forgotten just how long it is since I did leave? I haven't. It's ten days. Two hundred and forty hours and God knows how many minutes, all of them spent loving you and wanting you and hoping against hope that you'd come after me or ring or write. Or any bloody damned thing!'

His hands shot out to grab her, his face suffused with anger and violent emotion. 'You don't know the meaning of love, woman. Love doesn't take a man's pride and grind him into the dust. Love doesn't leave a man for days without a single word of contact. Love doesn't make a man despair that he'll never have children because the only woman he wants as their mother refuses to have them!'

He threw her from him then, turning away to ram closed fists down on the desk before whirling back to glare at her. 'Get out of here,' he muttered. 'Get out before I do something I'll really regret.'

Adrianna glared right back at him, her heart pounding, her mind exploding with an answering fury. 'Don't you speak to me like that, Bryce McLean! And don't you dare speak to me of regret! I know more about regret at this moment than you do. I regret ever setting eyes on you. I certainly regret the moment I put my hand in yours back there at that gorge. And I infinitely regret coming here today. I came out of love for you, my crazy, hopeless love for you. And what have you done? You've just thrown that love right back in my face! Well, I'll keep it, thank you very much, and hopefully, next time, I might find a man who'll value it a bit more than you did!'

She turned then and stalked towards the door, head held high, her pride intact but her heart breaking into a million jagged pieces.

'Don't go!' Bryce called in a haunted, desperate voice that tore at her very soul.

She stopped for a second, then walked on.

The air in the room moved like a rushing wind as he raced to grab her, spinning her round and holding her captive against the door. 'I can't let you go,' he ground out, wild eyes roving madly over her startled face. 'I love you, Adrianna. I can't live without you. These last ten days have been hell. Hell, I tell you!' Suddenly his hands were in her hair and he was kissing her, hungrily, desperately. 'Tell me what you want,' he rasped. 'I'll give it to you. Tell me what I have to do... I'll do it!'

He groaned, and pressed hot lips to the madly beating pulse at the base of her throat.

Adrianna was breathless, both with shock and a quickly rising passion. Already her hands had stolen to his hair and she was pressing his mouth to her rapidly heating flesh, but when his hands began to fumble with the front buttons on the dress, she tried to push him away. 'No,' she gasped. 'No!' She couldn't let him waylay her with sex when there was so much still to be settled.

He stopped, but didn't let her go, his eyes determined and quite ruthless as he stared down at her. 'This is the last time you're going to say no to me, Adrianna,' he said, striking fear into her heart till a surprisingly gentle smile softened his face. He led her over to the large brown armchair, drawing her down into his lap as he sat down in it. 'Now,' he said, 'let's get all this sorted out. You love me?' he asked.

She nodded.

'And you'll marry me?'

Again she nodded.

'And you'll have my children?'

She smiled, thinking to herself that she hadn't forgotten what he had said a moment ago, all the concessions he was prepared to make. 'How many would you like?'

His sigh was deep and contented. 'Then what were we arguing about?'

'What indeed?' Her eyes were innocently wide.

His narrowed. 'What sneaky plan have you got up your sleeve, Adrianna Winslow?'

She took his hands and ran them up and down her bare arms. 'Not a thing, as you can see,' she said seductively.

He laughed. 'You can't fool me, city girl. I've got your measure.'

She only smiled at this, but made no further move to stop him when his hands returned to the buttons on her dress.

'It was nice of you to invite Alan to our wedding, Bryce,' Adrianna murmured.

'He's not such a bad bloke,' came the grudging reply. 'He's changed.'

'You're only saying that because you know now that I never loved him.'

'Mmm.'

'Did you see how his ward gazed adoringly at him when he wasn't looking? If she's not in love with him I'll eat my hat. And wasn't Alan awfully sweet to her when she spilled that drink on her dress?'

'What an incurable romantic you are, Adrianna!' her husband grinned.

'I just want Alan and Ebony to be as happy as we are.'

'Don't you worry about Alan Carstairs,' Bryce said, smothering a yawn. 'He's not the type of man to ever come out on the losing end.'

Adrianna lifted her head from Bryce's stomach to look at him. 'You're not going to sleep, are you?'

'Now why would I do that? It's only three in the morning, we've been going since dawn, what with the wedding at Dover Downs, then the reception, then the flight to Sydney, and we've only been making love continuously since we arrived at the honeymoon suite here around midnight.'

'Well, we want to be sure, don't we?' she pointed out reasonably. 'After all, today's one of my best days to conceive. I worked it out on my calendar.'

Bryce groaned. 'I said I wanted children, Adrianna. I didn't mean I want one nine months to the day after our wedding night!'

'The sooner we start trying, the better. It might take months before I fall pregnant!'

'I certainly hope so. I want you all to myself for a while. The only person I want waking you in the middle of the night is *me*!'

She kissed her way up his chest and hovered her mouth above his. 'And why would you want to wake

me in the middle of the night, my darling sex
husband?'

'God only knows. With you I can imagine I'm goin
to need all the sleep I can get!'

'You're to blame,' she said, kissing him lightly o
the mouth. 'You've turned me into a sex maniac.'

'*Now* she tells me!'

She kissed his mouth again, then his throat, the
laid her head on his chest, sighing contentedly. 'It wa
a wonderful wedding, wasn't it?' she said softly.

'Mmm.'

'Mum likes you.'

'Mmm.'

'Even my rotten brothers like you. Though I ca
understand why. You shouldn't have bought them tha
cleaning business, you know—they don't deserve it

'Everyone deserves a chance, Adrianna. It's up t
them to take it or not. Besides, it's only money.'

Adrianna could only admire Bryce's attitude t
money. Enough was enough, was his motto. And the
both had more than enough, he said. Why not sprea
it around a little?

'I love you, Bryce McLean,' she said simply. 'S
much that I'm prepared to forgive you for once bein
a ladies' man.'

He laughed. 'What makes you so sure anything'
changed?'

Her hand slid down his body to enclose him in
rather intimate hold. 'But it has, hasn't it, darling?
she threatened with smiling teeth.

He paled for a moment. 'You wouldn't dare.'

'Oh, wouldn't I?' Her hand began to tighten. 'Hov
about telling exactly what you did get up to all thos
years ago when you were cavorting around lik
Sydney's answer to Casanova?'

'If I confess will you have mercy on me?'

'I might.'

'OK—well, back in the old days I started with the brunettes, then I moved on to the redheads, and finally I polished off all the blondes. Present company excluded, of course.'

'Bryce! I'm not amused.'

'Neither am I, my dear. Neither am I...' Suddenly he tickled her, then whipped out from under her loosening grasp to pin her laughing body to the mattress with his huge body.

'Help!' she squawked. 'You're squashing me!'

'Good. Now that I have you at *my* mercy let me point out that I don't fancy being given the third degree about what's well and truly over. I'm not interested in knowing your past conquests, Adrianna. I suggest you take a leaf out of my book. The present is what I'm concerned about. The present and the future. But, just to put that jealous little heart of yours at ease once and for all, let me assure you that I didn't bed all those ladies I dated. As a sweet and wholesome country lad I was quite content to give most of them a kiss and a cuddle. Admittedly, there were one or two that progressed further, but...'

'Only one or two?' she queried sceptically.

'OK, three or four. Who's counting?'

'*I* am!'

'Then make it five.'

'Five?' she echoed.

'You wouldn't have wanted me inexperienced, would you?'

'No.'

He heaved a sigh of mock relief. 'I'm glad that's all settled, then.'

'Hold your horses! What about since then? Who's been gracing those cool sheets of yours just lately?'

'Good grief, Adrianna! Do you also want to know what I've had for breakfast every day of my life as well?'

'No. Just every female you've had!'

He laughed. 'Then I'm afraid you'll have to learn to live with ignorance. I have no intention of giving you a blow-by-blow description of my past love-life. All I'm going to say is there was no female for nearly twelve months before you.'

'No one?'

'No one,' he pronounced firmly.

Adrianna was amazed. She was also pleased at the way Bryce always stood up to her. She had fallen in love with him when he was at his masterful worst, and underneath, she didn't really want him to change, for she admired his decisiveness, his strength, his slightly dominating maleness. But neither was she about to change either. 'Pull the other leg, Bryce McLean,' she countered drily.

'Scout's honour,' he insisted.

'Really?'

'Really. Even a suspicious woman like you has to concede that women aren't exactly thick on the ground around Dover Downs. And before you say it, no, I've never bedded Helen either. Not that she isn't an attractive girl, but I've known her all my life and I've always looked on her more as a kid sister than an available female. Mostly, since coming back to manage the station, I've restricted myself to the odd holiday affair, that's all. Funnily enough, as you get older, sex without love loses its appeal. But when I met you, my lovely siren . . . My God, I was climbing the walls in no time!'

He cradled her face and kissed her lightly. Then not so lightly. 'I will never want anyone else other than you, Adrianna,' he said huskily. 'Never. I love you to distraction. Forget about the past. The past is over, for both you and me. Today is the first day of the rest of our lives.'

Adrianna's heart turned over with happiness at the thought of living the rest of her life with this wonderful man. What would his children be like? she wondered, the thought still having the power to move her that if she had never met Bryce, never fallen in love with him, she wouldn't ever have even contemplated having a child. Now the idea was a driving force inside her, a goal that would give her more satisfaction than any career move ever could.

'And now,' Bryce murmured, 'where was I?'

Her movements beneath him were both direct and tantalising. 'You were just about to put those wonderful words of yours into action.'

His laughter was low and sexy. 'You've got a one-track mind, do you know that?'

'Yes.'

He gave a mock sigh. 'We husbands have it hard.'

'I hope so,' she smiled.

'Adrianna! You're wicked!'

'Not wicked, my darling. Just in love, in love with the most fantastic, sexiest man in the whole wide world!'

HARLEQUIN PRESENTS®

A Year
DOWN UNDER

WORDFIND #6

A	U	S	T	R	U	A	L	I	A	N	C	W	E	P
S	D	S	R	O	T	I	A	T	R	T	U	E	E	L
C	G	R	O	J	D	E	Y	Y	S	D	W	G	B	R
V	H	T	I	A	E	H	U	C	E	B	R	Y	C	E
R	H	Y	P	A	R	S	O	E	D	F	G	H	K	S
T	U	U	M	A	N	O	N	W	S	S	D	V	B	C
H	I	K	I	K	E	N	C	A	R	B	W	A	A	U
J	L	L	R	L	K	C	N	U	B	T	U	O	B	E
U	M	T	A	P	U	U	J	E	R	R	H	B	N	M
T	O	E	N	J	L	O	I	F	C	A	F	H	H	H
R	P	O	D	N	I	L	I	T	N	U	U	G	M	B
E	E	T	A	M	J	C	W	N	I	M	H	I	O	E
W	E	P	D	E	C	C	J	J	R	A	W	S	F	G
Q	E	P	D	M	C	L	C	L	E	A	N	C	V	B

ADRIANNA	MAN
AUSTRALIAN	MCCLEAN
BRYCE	MIRANDA
DESERT	OUTBACK
INTIMATE	RESCUE
LEE	TRAUMA

**Look for A YEAR DOWN UNDER Wordfind #7
in July's Harlequin Presents #1570
NO RISKS, NO PRIZES by Emma Darcy**

WF6

New York Times Bestselling Author

Sandra Brown

Tomorrow's Promise

She cherished the memory
of love but was consumed
by a new passion too
fierce to ignore.

For Keely Preston, the memory of her husband
Mark has been frozen in time since the day he was
listed as missing in action. And now, twelve years
later, twenty-six men listed as MIA have been
found.

Keely's torn between hope for Mark and despair
for herself. Because now, after all the years of
waiting, she has met another man!

**Don't miss TOMORROW'S PROMISE by
SANDRA BROWN.**

**Available in June wherever Harlequin
books are sold.**

TP

Relive the romance...
Harlequin and Silhouette
are proud to present

by Request

A program of collections of three complete novels by the most requested authors with the most requested themes. Be sure to look for one volume each month with three complete novels by top name authors.

In June: **NINE MONTHS** Penny Jordan
Stella Cameron
Janice Kaiser

Three women pregnant and alone. But a lot can happen in nine months!

In July: **DADDY'S HOME** Kristin James
Naomi Horton
Mary Lynn Baxter

Daddy's Home... and his presence is long overdue!

In August: **FORGOTTEN PAST** Barbara Kaye
Pamela Browning
Nancy Martin

Do you dare to create a future if you've forgotten the past?

Available at your favorite retail outlet.

HARLEQUIN Silhouette

REQ-G

Discover the glorious triumph of three
extraordinary couples fueled by a powerful
passion to defy the past in

Lingering Shadows

The dramatic story of six fascinating men and
women who find the strength to step out of the
shadows and into the light of a passionate future.

Linked by relentless ambition and by desire, each
must confront private demons in a riveting struggle
for power. Together they must find the strength to
emerge from the lingering shadows of the past, into
the dawning promise of the future.

Look for this powerful new blockbuster by *New
York Times* bestselling author

PENNY
JORDAN

Available in August at your favorite retail outlet.

PJLS93

HARLEQUIN PRESENTS®

A Year
DOWN UNDER

In 1993, Harlequin Presents celebrates the land down under. In July, let us take you to Sydney, Australia, in **NO RISKS, NO PRIZES** by Emma Darcy, Harlequin Presents #1570.

Eden wants it all—love, marriage, motherhood *and* Luke Selby. And not necessarily in that order. Luke doesn't believe in marriage, and fatherhood certainly isn't high on the handsome Australian's list of priorities. But he does want Eden. Dare they risk the price to gain the prize?

Share the adventure—and the romance— of A Year Down Under!

Available wherever Harlequin books are sold.

SOLUTIONS TO
WORDFIND #6

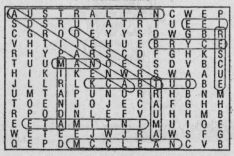

YDU-JNA